SYMPHONY IN INDIGO

Little Wolf

Copyright © 2019 Angela Timms

All rights reserved.

ISBN: 9781070344782

DEDICATION

For Mum & Dad.

As above, then as below
Who can guess where we will go
If we are naughty, or we are nice
Then some I guess will pay the price

Organic silver, hull so strong
Shooting earthbound, it won't take long
To get here finally, to put things right
And I'd put some money on it
There will be a fight…

Johnny be good, Johnny be bad
Johnny be angry, Johnny be sad
Johnny wake up now, and get a life
A job, some money, perhaps a wife.

Within the darkness of reason
The ink drying in the pen
Unused and unwanted
A wasted opportunity
Wisdom not spread
Beauty not created

Unexplored meaning
Lost to a lost world
Redundant mystery
Pe-packed adrenaline
Replaces thought driven
Out of space and time

Fingers fly on tiny box
While pens lay idle
Lost gift of individuality
Symbol of that which was
Out of sight, out of mind
Free speech unmonitored…

As ancient words do come to mind
The right passages we have to find

OTHER BOOKS BY THIS AUTHOR

The Eden Dream
Phoenix Rising: The Covenant
Phoenix Rising: Broken Vow
Thunder in the Mountains
No Strings Attached

ACKNOWLEDGMENTS

Thank you world for your inspiration, your darkness, your spite, your love, your happiness, a cacophony of everything.

Thank you Kevin Clarke, there at the beginning

Whispers in a wondrous world
Eternal beyond, life and hopes
Waking moment, celestial sleep
Shadows lengthen, light and mist

Shall we question all that is?
Because we must or don't understand?
What there is or what can be
Eternally changing

1

DREAM WEAVER, CRAVING SOLACE OF THE SKY

The mist crept over the field. Blades of grass disappeared in its milky smoothness. The world disappeared into a mystical miasma of swirling whiteness. It looked magical.

The Weaver of Dreams raised her golden scaly head and looked down over the land, she stretched her wings and folded them.

The old castle spread out before her and deep down she wished it was still that, a castle full of people with hopes, dreams and all the wonderfully complicated things that made them so interesting. She would have brought them such dreams.

The grass lay silent, a single rabbit bounced across and disappeared into the woodland. His white tail flashing as he went, then he was gone.

Such dreams, such hopes but the world did feel hopeless. Without hope, without dreams, without magic. Despite all that they had done the pages turned but they were empty of the magic that once filled every hill and dell. People didn't dream anymore, they didn't hope, everything was brought to them pre-packaged and explained, the unexplained discarded as some sort of hallucination or definitely something they would never mention.

She curled her sinuous neck and looked over the woodland. Where once people had imagined or seen woodland sprites now they saw practicality, woodland management and Ash Dieback.

Was this a world she could live with? Had they been wrong to bring her back? Even she could feel the dark despair that gripped the soul of mankind. Where laughter should ring out there was only sadness, complaint and a diatribe of bile. She felt like roaring, but that would wake everyone and the shockwave it would cause would give them even more to moan about.

Cry, she could do that. She could reach out but when she did she found only hate and spite. Even her spirits, the Frixians lay silent, their message unheard. They returned but will they stay? What they see and hear, who knows? The world is worth it but is humanity?

Their keeper sat at the keyboard, tapping out the mysteries as she put them in her tired brain. The day was long, it had to be, so much to fit in. Early to write, then the animals, then the other chores that had to be done. Each undertaken with a belief. That was her hope, that was where her dreams were kept alive. Somehow, out of the hatred came the last thing in the box, hope.

A whisper, quiet as smoke, no dreams, no hope, daring to dream but dreams dashed by spiteful hatred. She can feel it, she could scream. Her claws furled and unfurled, digging deep into the loamy soil of her new forest home. Around her the green buds of spring has burst into summer's symphony of green. She should be rejoicing. That pleasure too had been taken from her.

She felt it all, she saw it all, she wanted to act but couldn't. The time of dragons is spent. Fearful practicality grips the heart of men now. Greed, spite and vengeance for perceived wrongs without the intellect to know the reality, without understanding, without the acumen to listen and understand. An endless road to destruction.

> Dream thief, you steal my dreams
> Making all mundane and empty
> In the dark silence of the night
> For silence is what you seek
> When all is loud and chaos
>
> Dream thief you cannot win
> For a dream is eternally ethereal
> It slips through bonds and broken hearts
> It darkens the fierce burn
> It lightens the darkest night
>
> Dream thief you only borrow
> Keeping safe the dreams
> When life screams frantically
> Pointlessly extinguishing what can't be broken
> Before in the silence the dreams return.

> Words, lost in a moment
> Hoped for by the lost
> We can hope to be better loved
> Or we can love better.

The mist would clear but the situation would be the same. She knew that. The green magnificence of all around her, pointlessly trapped in darkness, she could feel it. The point where you see it but you cease to care, to feel, to hope. The blackness closes in and all beauty is for nothing. Why? She has to question, who wouldn't?

Silently she takes flight, her wings spreading and catching the spiritual winds. She soars into the blue sky, fluffy white clouds her backdrop, the estuary crawling its way to the sea, history lost. Carmarthen, the town spreads, oldest town in Wales, memories, she can feel them. Old and new. Found and lost.

Beneath her she feels it, the hatred, coming from the old wreck of a house, its heart ripped out, skin peeled, filled with bile and spite. She pulls back her neck, it would be so, so easy, to wipe the venom from existence and send it to oblivion. She must not. That is the line which must not be crossed, they are the devil's temptation. They are the evil which brings spite to the wonder of the world, personified. Her mouth shuts as she rises through cloud, through the atmosphere to spin into space.

Serene she hangs in the nothingness of the stars and looks back on the tired world. A battered and exploited ball spinning in space. A million hopes and dreams, a potential smashed and battered by man's greed. That original sin? Knowledge without wisdom. At poison chalice which was given where it should not have been. From the happiness of the "garden" to the self-created treadmill of the end game. The haves and have nots are reversed, those who have are those who need nothing more, those who have not will be eternally seeking to fill that unfillable cup.

> Thoughts and dreams unbound, chasing reality
> Steadfastly stalwart against the winds of fate
> A whirlpool of regret, fear, caution encouraged
> Sadness mixed with confusion and faith
> Whispers of the ethereal world, lost in the cacophony

Seeking again the solace of ethereal bliss
Quiet moments bringing answers
Projected angst of others' paranoia

She sighed, her heart pounding from the emotions she felt as she plummeted back to earth. The eternity of space was for another day, her charge was below her and she would never forget. A tiny hand, a Frixian' beauty, love without regret, giving without need for reward. One word brought her back, a name, "Widget". That tiny puppet, that huge spirit confined and helpless. But, that love was enough.

Her hopes and dreams, their hopes and dreams and the tiny souls who shared their table. Her plans were dashed against the rocks of despair, for now. One thing was certain, the old one wouldn't give up, and if the Old One, her Little Wolf wouldn't give up, how could she? The evening star that shone down on that little one had made her prove again and again that her heart was true. Little Wolf walked a lonely road, far from home though she had a place to be, but she walked it and when broken she crawled.

That spark, that belief and she knew that Little Wolf would find a way. In spite of, despite the spite of those who are spiteful. History is just that, the warnings are there. Humanity in microcosm, the bad and the bad. All that should be good brought bad by pre-planned agendas of those who had not the wisdom to question their wishes or deeds. In seeking to destroy in the name of their personal creation of what they think should be so they became the devil's puppets. In their seeking to destroy what they believed to be they created what they feared most. By their actions which were distractions to already overworked hands they created the very situation they had imagined. Manifestation in its purest form. They had a dread of the reflection of depression, the depression they had caused which manifested in the reflection.

Well she had puppets too, the freedom she gave was strength not weakness. The path isn't set, the future too. She sighed, breathing in the tainted air. One day...

The horror of what was, brought about by the actions of others. Easy to blame but when no understanding was requested or required there was no solace to be offered and all the truth in the world was not enough. Raining down their evil onto tormented souls who, after years of servitude were merely seeking solace but finding all that is bad in humanity, unfair? Just another test where no test was required, a wild card unplanned. Little Wolf came to find peace and dreams and hope for others, she found only war from those who had no comprehension or understanding.

Tears fall, pointless tears unneeded. This should not be.

Little Wolf was sleeping, a dreamless wasteland of broken thoughts and life laying in concrete encasement. Nobody is free now, the gift she sought to give brought to an unopen door by the actions of others. The history of it, laying bare. Why? That is the question, why? Why does mankind do anything? Man "kind", what a misnomer for a warlike race who has hardly evolved past caveman. Seeking to club, to own, to possess and if someone has something they do not bless that person and be pleased for what they have and for what others have worked so hard for. They seek to damage and break and control. What they do not know they make up and what they believe they believe beyond reason without question as to why though assuming without knowledge of the why.

Little Wolf came to find peace after lifetimes of war, she found only war and a war she had to win for the peace of others. A war she was too tired to fight but the old warrior had to find her armor of faith, her sword of truth and her shield of the love and protection she sought to bring for others. She would fight again, though it was so, so unfair. This was the pointless fight after all the point-ful ones she'd fought over time.

The Winter King, brought to despair and frustration by slithering actions of the deceitful. The impotence of dealing with vile evil without the ability to deal with it swiftly and cleanly. Not a battle that is allowed to be fought fairly, bound by law and the rules of a new age his hands are tied, he knows it, he acts on it and where those strike out he must stand strong, not strike back. Trusting to that same justice which is in the hands of others who have their rules to follow. Will they stand true to what should be? Are they the devil's pawns and will they also seek to bring things down?

Little Wolf sits in the desolation of what was done. The inevitable end of the beginning but beginning of the new. Words unheard, un-listened to. The why unimportant when the why is the most important.

Those who slithered in the darkness saw a woman, not the truth. They sought to drive her from the reality of what is and will be. The ship was still flying true despite the temporary failure. It didn't fail, it had seen worse, or better, depending on your point of view.

Memories might fade but the darkness and bleak nothingness of the lights going out in a tunnel, crowded with people below tons of rock and offices. That dreaded announcement of yet another bomb scare, yet another walk to the surface or hope that the train would move from its dark tomb to the next lit station before the vipers struck. Hope that it was just that, a scare.

Moments, not lost in time. Ticking away in silence when even a watch is heard on what was once a busy street. That silence after the desolation, so many miles away but so close when it is people on the end of a phone, dying in the fires or leaping from the tall buildings. What can you cling to? Thanksgiving that a grandfather didn't take that job and it wasn't you in those towers or sorrow for the someone who took what could have been your place. All gone, bone, ash and pain.

Everything changed, every moment ticked away differently after that day. A step outside the office into the sparkling greyness of the city street where there was silence. Silent hearts and no voices crying, it was like the mute button had been pressed. Steps followed known paths but as they descended to the bowels of the earth down familiar paths they were no longer familiar. Everything looked and felt different.

Strength and faith tested to the limit has it had been so many times before. So many others who sought to voice their views through the suffering of others. The fallout being those who learnt fear. So many years of the anguish of fear that other's beliefs would lead to pain, maiming, life changed in an instant. But this was different, this was something more.

It changed everything. Never again would an evening of bright lights, good food and good company not be marred by fear, caution and that need for observation that was reminded at every turn by announcements. Never again would that place of wonder hold any magic, the magic had gone. Where all was curiosity, art and beauty it became darkness. Noticing more? Seeing more? People, dark people, hanging around on corners, waiting, looking. No more the potential friend. Anyone with a backpack…

The day the world changed. The step by step walk down into the earth came with the fear that no IRA bomber had ever been able to strike. The nerves all struck at once, bleak faces who hardly looked at each other, a cacophony of strangers who sought no solace now with smiles. No smiles that day. Pity the man with the backpack and the dusky complexion. Not his fault but suddenly a solitary student was the source of everyone's fear. Unstated, we knew it, he knew it. Uneasy peace, uncertain forgiveness for a crime he hadn't committed or one he might?

Courage failed her, the doors opened at the station and she fled. Not in haste, made to look like it was the right station, the right place but there was a long walk ahead as there was no road back down into that bleak tunnel pressed together with so many others in the potential total darkness.

There was no happy walk that day, not curious look at all around, head down, foot by foot, step by step. The day the world changed forever.

Deep breath, the over ground train trundled into the station where other faces were lost in the crowd. Step by step up a street walked since childhood, familiar comfort in a crazy world. The day the world changed.

The news showed it all in glorious colour over and over again. She sat, making jewellery as she often did, over and over again, as if the action that was so normal would make it all go away.

The house was just so, just as she'd created it, rewired it, recreated a beauty that may not have been there to start with. Everything just so. New and improved, now a hollow box. No light there that day, just the echoes of the news and the certain knowledge that when the sun came up on the next day it would be no different.

Tears fell like rain for the lost and lonely, lost to death, lonely not to see those loved ones again. The darkness closed in. The almost never ending stream of the dead walking down a cobbled street with those who cared watching them, holding lanterns to show their way. So many people which tailed off to just a few, then one by one as those who didn't make it went to join their colleagues on the road to their future.

The day the world changed. It crawled on, days passed but it was never the same. Decision made, step taken, mistakes made out of fear and anguish and that absolute dread of the darkness every day. London left far behind for the wonders of Devon and the beauty of a harbour town full of magic and so, so far from the darkness of before.

It couldn't last, it shouldn't last. An impossible dream of green and trees built on a shaky foundation of another's arrogance and unwillingness to bend.

The days became years, with stories and possible futures leading back to the return, literally to the job that had been left. Like returning to a family much loved and much missed. But temporary, that was known, the day the world changed. It was never the same and then it happened again and that was the final step. The final challenge, the world sunk into an ever darker swamp of other's beliefs. The God of Love My Shepherd Is, he led Little Wolf to green pastures, by accident, by faith, by duty. Guiding her hand to a place far from the madding crowd where she could forget. A place where she could feel the wind on her face and the grass under her feet. The years rolled on but the place was not right, the challenges of altitude too great for the task that needed to be accomplished. Love and faith can do nothing against wind and the inability to grow things.

Stone walls encased, closed in. Dark and hard and difficult when there were too many people there. A lot had changed the day the world changed. So Little Wolf made a decision, a choice. It was a respite from the worry and constant financial drain of maintaining ancient stone, it was not so much outside the box as in it. Little Wolf saw the practicality of the situation, the hope that lay in that photograph of bleak grey barns and very little else.

Nothing was seen when the visit was made. Just a feeling. Those towering barns had such hope for so much. Not just her hope and dream, this was part of something far bigger. She knew it but was too tired to even care. Decision made, money slapped on theoretical tables and the path was undertaken.

It was a curious choice for one who had seen such gilded halls and sparkly chandeliers. It was a simple choice of what was important. Let the halls be living wood. Let the dining room be the open sky. Let walls not encase or drag her into the darkness that she feared so much now. Let nature be her home, the box just a place to keep out of the rain and put her head down when there was nowhere else to be.

So many houses made "just so" but rarely seen due to prior engagements. So many houses made "just so" to be left just as quickly on the road to the final location.

Much loved places labored over to perfection. A lifetime of decoration and soft furnishings all worked, chosen and placed to that final Symphony in Velvet. That moment of sitting, job done in a place that needed no more work, no more effort and which reflected the soul sufficiently that it was a calm place to sit and be and look and feel without the need to think of more.

That was the old world, but the old world had changed. The new world had no sense, it had no place for the days of fun and the evenings spent in places with gleeful chatter and fine food. It had no place, destiny was calling and the gauntlet thrown down. She took it up, not so much gladly but she took it.

The step was taken, the wheels turned, hoof and paw loaded and unloaded and the engines shut down. This was it. A new Eden.

Water, none of it. Power, none of it. Hope, plenty of it.

Water, plenty of it in truth. Huge roof expanses provided a deluge of water every time it rained. The concrete blissfully relieved from its regular dousing. Plastic encased in IBC tank it prepared itself for its tasks ahead.

Challenges were a plenty, mostly the washing machine but that was a simple one, if you think outside the box. If water goes in, it can go in. If the pressure wasn't great enough, use a bucket. Job done, or rather washing done.

A spring provided more, if more was needed. Gleefully met with enthusiasm but apathy set in when more was provided than was needed. Why struggle up the hill with water when so much just landed. A second tank, purchased, filled but not needed. Finally moved for ease of goat watering. Their own thousand liters.

Power, that had to be had. A single, simple solar panel. Nowhere near what was needed for comfort, just a small test case which proved to be enough. It took working, manipulating the day and a generator. It could have been permanent with a few extra panels but the power supply was sort of there anyway. It was a natural progression that when offered a reconnection and the reconnection not needed the next step was to get pylons and cables taken underground. The view was no longer marred by them and the yard blissfully free of them.

The spiteful venom of that first day that the neighbor demanded the shut off was a distant memory from a practical point of view but the memory of the uncouth greeting will stay forever. It didn't just colour everything, it was indicative of form and meaning from their point of view. Demanding and enforcing their views on what they felt were lesser beings. The only chance to make a first impression evaporated in the need for dominance and practical enquiry rather than friendly greeting and right footedness.

Try again later with a lie that the water was a surprise to them, made foolish by the request for an early shut off via the solicitor and compounded by mentioning a notice of disconnection. Something not possible with a private pipe and a private disconnection.

Nobody had foreseen that the water could not be reconnected but the lack of possible discussion did mean the impossibility of any of these things being sorted out without a drastic cut off.

All problems were sorted out but the scene was set for future transgressions of Little Wolf's peace and right to a happy home.

Privacy was attacked next as all undergrowth which had given privacy was swept away to the degree of using a digger. So much for the solitude of the Zen Garden and the ugly old caravan was exposed in all its non glory which was a mystification. If anyone would question it was obvious and played out pretty soon after a new abode was dragged somewhat unwillingly onto site that the dragging back was to provide the sort of view that could be complained about. Thereby came the lesson that situations were created later to be used.

To list the transgressions intended to lessen the spirit and cause an evacuation would be pointless.

Suffice to say that anger was needed where depression had set in. Time passed, slitherers slithered and sought to drive her from her home. Attacks like a time of old. There was a time that walls were a bastion, without those walls the slitherers could get in without hindrance. Haste overtook esthetics and the ensuing Mad Maxification of the vicinity of the fence in question was artistic in its own bleakness.

The day after the Winter Wolf left her side the sun shone from the sky as the evil one slipped unseen into the yard. His intent wicked, his soul damaged by the actions he was about to commit. The lack of understanding his downfall, the innocent a sacrifice on the altar of his avarice.

A wanton boot which split and sundered the dog door of the major hound allowed the enmity of days of bouncing outside and the opportunity to encroach on the old master's territory just too much for the spirited spaniel. He paid the price for his crossing of the boundary but the guilt lay with the one who had permitted the gate so carefully placed for the protection of all to be damaged and left in such a state.

Blood on the ashes, as that dear one went to the fire the spiritual sword was picked up again. The mists of doubt gone. The wolves howled, one of their pack gone, an innocent one. They howled and they will howl again so that the guilty may hear them. That ancient cry, baying for blood but held by the resounding strength of truth and justice.

> Time and again, through time
> Ancient ones speak through us
> There is more, some do seek it
> Now is the time, before all is lost
>
> I can't be alone in knowing
> Keeping seeds we should be sowing
> Building a world where things will grow
> Micro climate, generation
> Not reliant on a breaking world
> Time is fleeting
> Time for greeting
> Not a time to stand alone.

The Weaver smiled as Little Wolf wrote, ink on paper, the word spread but would the ideal? That depended on how far humanity had gone from that which it could have been in those green fields all those years ago…

Her Warrior unbroken…

2

Calling…
A silent bell rings
Answer?
At what cost?
Do it now,
Time is fleeting
Or much later
All is lost

Early morning
Thoughts are calling
Memories falling
Into place

    Little Wolf was writing, sitting in the solitude, a momentary respite in the chaos that was caused by others. Around her the Mother kept things going, as it always had been. She too cried for the trapped loved ones who could not run free lest the evil would harm them. She too knew the truth of it, the evil that is humanity. She too knew that some must wander far from the castle walls and they were the ones she could protect best she could.
    The ponies walked their path through the snow. Bodies chilled but warmed by their natural coat as nature intended. Their daily journey

done they sought to return to the gate where their warming food awaited.

Their way was blocked, the gate that had been open was now closed and there was no way home. Using her strength Ebony pushed, her black coat stark against the white snows of winter. She pushed with all that she had to get to that tasty food which would make life so much better, so hard that gate and lock bent but did not give way. Bill the Pony, his coat like the snow stood with her, his eyes wild and his pony anger real, there was a gate shut where before there had been none.

The night was cold and bleak ahead of them. They didn't understand, how could they?

A light in the darkness, a pinprick of hope, yellow on the glistening snow. Footsteps crunched the crystals to leave boot prints one by one. A track of hope, hand on the gate, the lock slider raised, the bolt pulled back, salvation. The gate swung open, the ponies galloped to the warmth of their bucket, evil foiled, they were safely fed.

The night passed, the next the evil one slithered to carry out his wicked deed, the gate shut again and again they were rescued. Little Wolf smiled, grabbing the metal gate she threw it from its hinges never to be shut again. In that action energy flowed into the Universe, for one injustice there will be a reaction, power in the darkness. Unbowed and untamed.

Little Wolf wandered in the snow, taken from the warmth of the box which was their protection. She had no care for that, her steed and her friend were safe.

The Weaver watched and listened, dipping into the thoughts, invasion of privacy but not a time for the feinting diamonds.

Why does anyone do anything? Everyone is a product of everything that has happened to them and their surroundings. Daily and even momentarily we are faced with choices, some so mundane we don't even think about them. All important. What if we chose not to take the next breath? Something so simple and mundane that we do over and over but if we don't do it the results are catastrophic.

In every situation we have to look at it as that, a situation. Sitting in the stillness after the temporary storm it is time to question. In an old world that questioning would be enough. Every situation is different and every situation should be evaluated as that situation, not as a textbook response to something that ticked a few boxes. The root cause is sometimes more important than the reaction. A broken creature will strike out in that moment of total darkness brought about by the actions of others. That creature is not evil, that creature is not wicked. More to be understood and pitied for the situation than to be hated and berated though berated is also necessary to eliminate that happening again. There is a huge difference between actions and reactions. What is needed is understanding.

> No need for conflict for the sake of it
> Ego-orientated competition is a waste of time
> Losing sight of what is important
> Petty disagreements put behind
> Seeking the ability to live one's ideals
> Combining artistry with integrity
> With the needs of the market place
>
> There is a need to ground now
> In the silence things make sense
> To help to avoid things
> And make things more along

There is the beauty of art and the reality of the real world. That is the balance.

There is a truth in this world that underlies the shadows cast over it by the deeds of man. The world is changing and a greater evil is creeping into the shadows and when it is strong enough it will step into the light. Insidious it corrupts thoughts and works towards its end, using good people who think they are doing good.

> Darkness all around us
> The evil that men do
> Counteracted by beauty
> And the love of me and you
> Nothing is forgotten
> Nothing left behind
> We will do our duty
> And a life will find

Man's nature is to be angry
Mankind's nature is to complain
Strike out for what is thought right
So in belief, right on both sides
Nobody can win
If only the big stick's views prevail
Reason is the weapon of choice
Goodness in men's answer is the answer
When only violence is the solution seen
There will be no solution
Only war and death
Squabbling over a dying Earth
Poisoning the patient
Arguing over her death bed
In the name of the Father
While the Mother cries

The circle of being
A blank slate
Tiny child
Mind eager for knowledge
Initial basic
Onion skin complicated
Built up over its ages
Until opinion and views it has
Tempered by love
Guided by wisdom
What we conceive is amorphous
What we create is conceptual
Lessons learnt
Doctrine delivered
Victim of circumstance
Human to follow
To swallow and believe

Spout learnt truth
In the shadow of a dying world
Where Angels fear to tread
The wisdom of ages
Encased in the modern issue
Bogged down in bureaucracy
Lost in a lost world
Where all have a view
Where few are silenced
But obsessed with trivia
And missing the point
They might as well be
Head fuddled by demands
Of the modern world
Where too much is known
And little is really understood
Names learnt like a mantra
Used like tools
Until reality dawns

Waiting on others
That's what we do
Choose your product
Get in the queue
Buy on line
One click its done
With that action
The need to see people is gone
Process packed
Isolation is yours
Designed and fashioned
So nobody cares
Fed with the views
Enough to debate
So they forget
That the world's in a state

They speak of Global Warming
But what of degrees?
Knocked off its axis
Come on, if you please
It will make a difference
A bit one of no doubt
So go on I say, take a look
If you haven't yet found out

I'm all for recycling
Green living one and all
But think of the tectonic plates
Before you make the world a football
Hard on the outside
Soft lava rests inside
Kick it and break it
And then you will find
A whole world of heating
Coming up from within
And the land you relied on
Will very soon be gone.

It depends on how you handle it
When bad things come around
A test of your control
A test of all you are
Stand up for who you can be
And don't let them dictate
With party manifestos
Write your own mandate.

Moments change everything
Nothing stays the same
From moment to moment
Whispers in the wind
A breeze moves a leaf
The view has changed
Sun touches soil
Unseen becomes seen

Cold becomes warm
If per chance
A seed will grow
Many years later
Another majestic tree
Will grace the planet
Will fill our lungs
With the breath we need
Remember…
All actions have reactions
All reactions have actions
So shall it be…

Wishes, screamed at the wind
Wants and desires
Oft not granted
Oft the wish is not intended
Not needed
The wish itself is the wish granted
The need that drives
Others are wishes needed
Deeply desired from the purity of the soul
Screamed to the ether by a needy heart
Manifested by the pure desire
Carried forward by the rightness
Created by an inspired dream
Granted in graciousness
Grateful recipient in a creating world

Peace in the soul
A wish beyond all others
Needed quiet for contemplation
Shadows awaken from quiet slumbers
Sultry seeking solace
Happiness in responsibility
Acceptance of all, and understanding
Abandoning dread in favor of solace
Shadows just shading
Seen as mystery, unlike shadows of the soul

Visions of another world
Momentary glimpses of magic
Seen in the shadows
Veils close not closed

Care tiny sparrow
Dark things lurk
Memories of an old world
Part remembered…

Rebel in a lost world
How can I scream of injustice?
When everyone screams now
Their right to comment
Wrongs no longer unnoticed
Their shock watered down
Dreams gone in a plethora of reality
Where everyone is different
In being differently the same
All becomes a grey soup of complaining
Where the complaints are forgotten
As the complainer moves on
Or adds to the repertoire
Where teenagers must rebel
To find their place in the world
To find their passion and purpose
That will shape their future reality
Per chance of duty and responsibility
Where the rebellious days
A guidance, or something to be forgotten?
Silent empty seats
Their once occupants never forgotten
The empty chair their epitaph
Absent friends
Gone forever
The seats forever empty
Other the years more seats will be empty
But so must it be
Or there would be no seats for new life

So has it been
The circle of life
Fair and unfair
Each mortal has their time
Tick tock
Never forever
Just a portion in time
Until it is over…

The past, set behind the future
Pushing it on and shaping
The unforged mind
As views are made
Tempered by experience
Fed by information, true or false
Found or given, fed or foraged
Assimilated into the growing entity
Which becomes adult
Then others must listen, right or wrong
Right in opinion, believing in fact
True is all there can be
Which truth though?
That is to be seen.

Everyone knows you
When it is your moment
Good or bad
They stand beside you
If fame is at your door
They will remember you
When you were forgotten before.

Odd it is
On the day that you die
They will know you more
Than they ever did
People who in passing
Have once heard your name
Reach back in memory

Recalling it all again
That special memory
Of someone who was never a friend.

Where are we going to?
What must we do?
We will do our duty
That much it true
But where will it take us?
What duty to find?
Then the past we will leave behind
Pointlessly doing things
That has no place
So from the darkness
We'll do an about face

The green of the woodland
We must protect
Making it powerful
That is the effect

In the silence
Gossamer wings fly again
Ancient spirits rise
From the dawn of time
To the end of it
Give mankind a reason
To respect the woods
To respect the world
To respect that which was
And will be again

Hope goes on
A flame that burns
Beyond devastation
The sun will come up
The sun will go down
On happiness or sad day
Time will pass

Nothing will be forgotten
Pain lessens
It doesn't go
Some days it comes back
Sharp as the day
The sun goes down
The sun comes up
Life goes on
For you to step back into
When the time is right.

Space and time to think
Free of the clutter of the modern world
As an excuse it is a good one
For we have no hunting to do
Armed when we leave our cave or cottage
Border disputes making life challenged
Life moves on
Day after day
Year after year
Progress or just different
The thoughts of woodland
Where no pixies roam
No longer the fear of the otherworld
So should they return?
No bears or wolves are at our door
Health and safety nightmares
More dangerous dangers these days
Laughingly petty but micro-analyzed bad
Where no greater danger is at your door.

Light, light come my way
Not for a moment, not just for a day
A happier life, where all is right
Not survival, no more of the blight

A positive future, built on faith
No more ghosts of the evil wraith
Belay the darkness, consign it away

So that I can enjoy a brighter day

Shun the darkness, don't give it power
Wash it away with a spiritual shower
The world is crazy, that's what I think
I ask you answers, lets see through the chink

Such dreams we dream in waking
Rounded by practicality
Vaguely escaping the confines of experience
Ever seeking something beyond
Ethereal as tendrils, creeping around reality
Feather light they weigh heavily on the trapped
Shackles that cannot be broken
Tradition and other's opinion
Head down and plod
But, per chance, dare to dream
To reach beyond the solitary existence
To a world beyond
To creativity, to hope and so much more
But, leaving the protective confines of a dream
So much doubt and the shifting sands
Of a world where there is no security
Where all depends on the whims of the populace
In an ever rigid world.

Small is beautiful
Unreached beyond its potential
Compact in its practicality
A world within words
Seeking that which is meant to be
Making dreams a reality
Seeking solace in silence
A cacophony of light and action
Stalwart in a fickle world
Tiny moments brought together
Where darkness and depression has no place
A silent calling
Most will ignore

Others will evade
Some will listen
And act
And be
Free…

Dreams are for sleeping
Where Morpheus calls us
To a world without constraint or form
Where everything is possible
Rounded by the space of a lifetime
Tomorrow, always tomorrow
When life is lived today
So all must be done
In the here and now
As time is fleeting
Flowing by as it must for all
Given like a gift
Wasted on trivia
Dashed hopes or evolution?
The show must go on
And it will
Inevitably.

Times past, future and present
Hold sway in a moment of decision
Bend or hold fast, either does if appropriate
Ink on paper
Seemingly innocuous
Unfettered by the confines of verse and structure
Life sucking into stricture's perimeter
Formulaic splendor or free speech?
Words, letters, flying about
As yet unformed, unclaimed
Free for the taking.

A page is potential
A single piece of paper
Like a life

There at the onset
Poised with anticipation
Captivated by potential
Awaiting influence
To fulfil its potential
Or rest idle or perchance trivially pass
To oblivion as a wasted note
Leaving nothing lasting
Just a page
That can last forever for what is there written
Or be
Just a page…

More time for leisure
Less money for leisure
Cycle and circle
Boredom makes darkness
In the creative mind
Where all must be and do
Leaving scars and a void
Need erased
In the rush to nowhere
Or the machine like machinations
Of another week
Seeking solace in silence
Or the clatter of the age
Great minds unfocused
Potential wasted
Machine code bliss
For the few
Mindless oblivion for the masses…

THE EDEN DREAM REVISITED

People live in a woodland
All about them is green
The earth provides their food
They will not starve
The land provides their water

They will not thirst
They have what they need
They have what is wanted
They have no dread of tomorrow
As they can live in the today
Unfettered by the needs of the modern world
Living with it, enjoying it
Having all the blessings of the modern age
Using technology to walk lightly
Living lightly with hope.
Words and writing
Future blighting
If negativity does creep in
Future glory, not a story
Truth rises through the din
Values not issues that it true
Holding to beliefs
Chitter chatter, loads of clatter
What you still can hear is true.

The first step is being on the same page
The next is having a page to be on
Walk your walk
Talk your talk
Deserve what you are given
Talked it, walked it, but only a bit

Ideas nip at my heels
Immobile and impotent
Costings and plans
Thoughts and ideals
As the year ticks on
No position to decide
Talk is cheap
But the gap is wide

Culture clash
Future smash
Grab for cash

Then they bash
In a flash
Peace is gone
All are one
When it's done
No more fun
In the sun.

So many days
So many ways
To get you through the day

Question and answer
To avoid disaster
Then onwards you do go.

A journey starts with a step. Be it just outside the door or to the furthest reaches of the old Empire. Just opening your eyes on a new day brings the magnificent expectation of what could be. Disappointment is possible but so too is a myriad of colourful experiences.

We are all about to embark on a great adventure. Unexpected in the decision perhaps but happy when made. From eye open to eye close, a new day.

Life is a journey. It starts with the first breath and ends with the last. Happy or sad, good news or bad. Each aspect makes up the whole. Every situation changes the individual. We are a product of what has happened to us. It is the strength of character that makes the difference between victim or someone who learns from the lesson.

Choices can be wrong but at the same time choices can never be wrong. Lessons are learnt for the future so that when it really matters the right choices can be made.

You can wish but what happens, happens. Manifestation is real though. String theory is why it has a scientific explanation. Even if you don't know what you want, deep down your spirit does. So being able to accept this and be grateful for the good that comes your way and making the most of it is important.

Effort is needed, as in all things. Faith and hard work. The right choices make it easier. If the choice is wrong then if you work out why it is wrong you will know how to put it right. It may not be wholly wrong, it could be partly wrong or your considering of it could be wrong and it could eventually end up right.

>Thoughts and stories often come
>Walking the lines of oblivion
>Clinging to the mind
>Music inspires
>It touches the soul
>It frees the mind
>To remember
>Words streaming
>Free beliefs and wishes
>Some caught in oblivious disaster
>Some dreaming the dream time
>More moments fragmented.
>Oh for the voice of silence
>The peace to quell the rain
>A thousand droplets, all or one
>So life can sprout anew
>Water still in harbours
>Crashing out at sea
>It only really matters
>When it relates to me
>For life it will continue
>Great machinations or quite small
>Great thoughts or really tiny ones
>When the future comes to call.

>Shadows creep around the periphery
>Clinging tenuously 'neath a stormy sky
>Slithering into spaces
>Reaching with impotent fingers
>Spreading dread to scare worn minds
>Empty threats, pointless fear
>They cannot exist without it
>So they are the ultimate portent of hope
>Like paranoia and fear of failure
>It exists because of the existence of hope

The fear of the lack of it.

Questions and answers
They co-exist and make each other
One without the other is pointless
Which comes first?
Does the question justify the answer?
Does it make it real?
The answer exists without the question
The question is there as we must know.

Art and form
Does form need purpose?
Fractious beauty in the eye of the beholder
Created out of creativity
Or the need for appreciation
Made out of want or need
Or made as art must..
A creative craving to be
Crawling from the creator's mind and demanding birth.
Knowledge and power
Confusion and misdirection
Spin doctoring and all curing information
Seeped out while the world is busy
Transfused from silent prison
To forgotten oblivion
Mentioned in passing
Then conveniently forgotten

The world turns
An independent ball
Un-insignificant (sic) moments reverb
Shockwave in the Universe
Evolution stunted by intelligence
Eyes are watching
Fearful
That the virus may not stay contained.

Carelessly left floating in space
Children running the kindergarten
The lunatics running the asylum
Individualistic individuals
Intelligently believing
What they have created to be right
Figures back it up
Motivated by motivationalists
The loud screams
The quiet explanation
Raggedyman complains
From his sack cloth seat
His voice made irrelevant
By his drug soaked depression
Self-fulfilling prophecy
Of the impotent intellectual fool

Rats like cattle
Fed a controlling diet
Information per-packed
Delivered in a pretty package
Results monitored and modified
They have their say
They have their rights
Do they?
Voices will not be silenced
Massive overload of jibberish
From the tent infested field
Wild weed wafts wantonly
Peace pipe of doomsayers
Toothless wonders satisfyingly sated
That they know their truth
That they speak the truth they are given

Happily providing a pre-packaged excuse
Solution being a problem to be a solution
Wrong people or right people
Wrong world or right world
Each to their own

Each to own or own nothing
Nothing to lose or gain
Information stacked in single backpack
Wafted by smoke and fire
Anger fuelled toothless wonder
Crawls back to his tent
Sated and satisfied
That his truth is spoken, sedition spread

Toothless wonder snapping at a mirror
Empty oblivion of rattle tabs
Prescribed portly providence
Peace in a bottle
Crawl into the shadows.

Words are spoken
Synapses snap, trap shut
Speak or listen
Truth wrapped in sensationalism
Understood or misappropriated
The secret stolen or given
Damp ammo launched abstractly
The ball spins in space
Once thought anonymity forgotten
As mistakes come to attention
Ball tipped mystery
Viewed, observed and noted
The virus has teeth
It looks to the universe
With hungry eyes
No longer contained
By immature machinations in the playground
Key market
New market
Shove it all on black
Track stacked
Fall back
Figures float around
Inter-preted, toys petted

Figures made of steel
Morph figures, transgressors
Statistics aren't ever real
Half full, half empty
Liquid, it moves on
Don't drink it, time'll shrink it
Eventually it's gone
Action, faction, reaction
Peace, pacification, pictureification
Needs wanted by all
Or the football monkeys will fall

Truth stands alone
Incorrupt and immoveable
Fact ammo deviates the projection
So everything can be true
Truth deviated by interpretation
Manipulated for peace or war
Anger at all or anger at nothing.

United world of wonder
People can't get on
Put them together
Nothing moves along
Can't agree on religion
On the name of a one god
Nothing is united
Nothing, all or said
The power it is out there
Sadly looking down
Letting children break it
Time perhaps to frown.

Sad anger, frustration
Thoughts made, too many to mention
Manipulated by anger
Creativity shred
Playful pastime
Pointlessly portrayed in endless chat

The End of the World
The end of all things
Silently slipping into oblivion
Damnation salvation
Forced to behave
Extinction guaranteed
Virus wipe out

The six seals are open
Riven by the sword
Wax seals unspoken
Theology seeping out
Coming on a fire cloud
The ship is revving up
Time to check up on us

Are we that important?
We rewrite all the words
The signs they are all out there
Old times they are long gone
Times of desolation
When all the faith is gone

Hollow earth and people
Created in a dish
Far too many people to feed, with just two fish.
Empty shells are angry
Vessels for the shard
Anger and selfish attitude
We could just discard
Too many people
The petri dish is full
Rates they are all hungry
So the truth they bend
Selfish satisfaction
Destruction has been lost
Where are the Angels who used to claim the cost?
Signs in the sky
The sun blotted out

By the big space ship
It was there at our birth
Our toys they are broken
Cast into a pit
There in their glory
On the pile they sit
Gluing and sticking
Then making more
Loving and caring
Is seen as a chore

Four horsemen of the apocalypse
Their horses are tacked up
The signs are all out there
If we would but see

2
TEAR FOR A DYING WORLD

The engine of the car fired up and the wheels turned. Valleys and mountains echoed with the ancients, towering over the tiny car on the ball of rock spinning in space.

A world in torment, forgotten for a moment as two women drove on a single quest. Thoughts belayed by conversation and a pleasant day's drive.

Task done and the road home laid out before them. One task done, the main one, the reason but in the reason there was the fulfilment. The journey was to bring a dog home, though the dog would never fulfil its purpose, it didn't have the ability it was brought home all the same as it was its destiny.

Darkness fell over a troubled world as the car came to a standstill. The choice wasn't one. For years the place had been a place to find, to go to, and in going the last of the old quest was complete. In a tiny lane off the main road the engine stopped. Memories of great battles, noble men and not so noble, the ages flew by in an instant as the great ones caught up with what had happened. They rested beneath the earth, ancient claws still, ancient wings furled but their eyes opened, they felt the Old One come.

A single tree, just an acorn when the world was yet old, now the sentinel, where the power lay dormant. By chance, by choice, by destiny. It's noble branches reaching to the sky, its roots deep into the earth, connecting earth to sky, connecting that which is above with that which slept below.

It had been years, many years, since the Dragon Lords had sat in that ancient cave at Dynas Emrys.

Vortigen had been having construction problems as his castle kept falling down every night because two dragon were warring underneath. Merlin offered his assistance and in legend the dragons were freed.

Something must have happened after that time as there were three dragons resting beneath that hill, sleeping. They were believed to be trapped but perhaps only trapped by the magic leaving the world and they had chosen to spend their exile together. The green, red and white had slept for many, many years and they slept now, one trapped by Merlin, two trapped by their own choice, saddened by a world that no longer needed them. Back then it had been a good thing, they stepped back to let the World of Men have its time. Now for the sake of the Mother they had to take wings and fly again. But they were trapped, that had been "the deal". At the last meeting of the Dragon Lords at Dynas Emrys they had laid aside their physical form and gone into a slumber.

In their dreams they still knew what was happening but their time of glory was passed. They were just memories, myths, legends, an unreality which was yet to be awoken.

> Bound in Stone
> His visions a world encompass
> Silent the dreaming visionary
> Has been lost for a century, an age
> Eternally waiting to be free again
> Free to fly on the wings of imagination
> Silently drifting on the edge of sleep
>
> Wistfully his jaws are silent now
> Pitifully his claws are encased in granite
> Enchained but his mind drifts free
> Silently touching and feeling the consciousness
> Of a thousand kindred spirits
> Who are lost in a lost world…

The engine stopped, prophecy fulfilled. The Old One and the Blonde One. To one the ancient gifts already known, to the other the riches of Merlin, gifted for her kindness of bringing the Old One to fulfil the destiny. Her gift was given, it was then her choice to unwrap it whenever she felt it was time. Some riches are greater than gold, some will last for a lifetime. One day she will look inside and find that treasure acquired on that night.

The Old One stepped from the car, no fear or hope, just a knowing and a journey fulfilled. The name had come to her long ago, the visit had been "on the list" but put off due to distance.

Only now "by accident" did she find herself here. Another journey the purpose, the purpose the journey.

She stepped out of the car and again the feelings came to her of what to do. She stepped onto the road, step by step she felt the tree, it called to her. As she had done so often before her hands touched ancient bark. She reached to the stars and ancient power flowed through her. She reached down into the earth and ancient earth power arose through her, the two met. Power entwined with power and flowed, down her arms, through her palms and her fingers. A tingling feeling the only sign that what she was doing was real.

The reality of it dawning, the fear, the hope, all wound into one. Memories of the images which came before. The red wax seals on ancient doors, riven by the sword given. Inside the dragon, the wisdom, the white powder, details lost but written in books she had, notebooks set aside for so many years as not deemed important back then. Images that the meaning were lost until realization dawned that they had been forgotten until they were needed. Needed now.

> Take me home, to the place I once knew
> Take me home
> To a place where the sky burnt with the brightness
> Of a thousand dreams
> To place where the air is pure
> And my heart beat with the melody of the ancients.
>
> Now I've come home, to the place I once knew
> Now I've come home
> To a place where the stars beam with a brightness
> Of a thousand dreams
> To a place where the air is not pure
> But my heart still beats with the melody of the ancients.

Light met with light, a myriad of splinters and shards, colours and white, all colours and none, spiraling upwards in a pillar of hope. Above and below connected in one glorious moment that only one could see perhaps. Across the world nothing changed. There was no great revelation and no great awakening. The pillar was glorious but momentary in the grand scheme of things and in time will be forgotten.

The energy reached down into the earth, breaking the ancient prison, smashing the shackles that had bound the willing. It was their time again.

As one the three took to the air her scales reflected the light, magical light and that of the spectrum. The white, the red, and the green, their wings spread over a dying world, bringing life, light and magic back.

Their wings flapped, stretched from many years of resting, their scaly heads looked around and they breathed, their fire, ice, power and nature mixed in a single beam which penetrated the earth, giving it back its ancient power.

Silence falls as a voice cries out in the darkness
Whispers are heard as fragile it is subtly silenced
Eternally its resonance radiates around the globe
Deafening it's almost silent message
Gently it touches war torn hearts
Hope a reason to live
Faith a reason to try
Joy a reason to laugh
Truth but still to cry

The moment, caught in the unwritten, unseen history of time, happened as it must and as it was foretold in the annals not known to man, not written or published for the prying mind. Part of the unseen world which touches and controls the other, lost control? The word, the wish, the intent, reclaiming its place.

Around the world in silent glens and forests ancient little things awoke and those already awake greeted their lost relatives and friends, so long gone. Tiny gossamer wings flittered around ancient trees, no leaves as yet but buds of spring awaiting to burst.

From trees and water sprites, nixies, pixies and dryads stretched ancient arms and craved solace of the sky. Craved sanctuary of the earth.

Concrete covered where some had once lived, these exiles moving

to what was left, welcomed by the denizens who found them space.
New woods claimed old spirits, there was still hope.

Watcher of the crashing sea
Worshiper of ancient majesty
Boundless slapping of watery wings
Ancient power unbound and free

Frozen in time
Whisper of eternity
They gave us a dream
But the dream was not mine

Through the night they drove as the dragons flew above, back to the ancient castle, forgotten, near Merlin's birthplace. The ancient and the new, coming together for the future.

The car drew to a halt, engine stopped and cooled and life went on but different. They knew about the dragons who flew down into the ancient woodlands and landed, wings folded as ancient spirits stepped out of very tree.

That night an ancient court was held. The Dragons took their place around the crest of the ampitheatre, joined by the Gold, the Weaver of Dreams, allowing the court of the fey to sit within the semi-circle. The kings and queens of the Fey, coming in from all areas to this ancient and untouched place to sit in court over a world they had not had a say in for so many years.

The History Keeper pulled in all of history and all things and played it out in a bubble above them. In under an hour of mortal time they were appraised of all that had happened, in all places at all times until they all knew everything.

Then they talked, and talked, and talked, through the night.

It was a time for a new order, a new time of dragons and fey, a time to bring back the magic to the world. Their justice would have to rule again, they could no longer stay silent. The bond was broken, the promise broken their time had come again.

Above the spirits watched, not displeased at the broken promise, it was necessary, outmoded and more detrimental than beneficial. They gave their blessing, unwanted and unasked for but necessary to them.

What was broken asunder was brought back together, the spirits of all worlds united in one purpose, to repair the damage done by the miscreant children.

>Oh for the voice of silence
>The peace to quell the rain
>A thousand droplets all or one
>So life can sprout anew
>Water still in harbours
>Crashing out at sea
>It only really matters
>When it relates to me
>For life it will continue
>Great machines or really quite small
>Great thoughts or really tiny ones
>When the future comes to call.

>Questions and answers
>They co-exist and make each other
>One without the other is pointless
>Which comes first?
>Does the question justify the answer?
>Does it make it real?
>The answer exists without the question
>The question is there as we much know
>But the biggest question of all
>Should we know.

>Art and form
>Does form need purpose?
>Fractious beauty in the eye of the beholder
>Created out of creativity
>Or the need for appreciation
>Made out of want or need
>Or made as art must
>A creature craving to be
>Crawling from the creator's mind
>Demanding it's birth

Steam, smoke and mirrors
Ethereal beliefs creating an ethereal world
Safely sanctified and contained
Faithfully funded
The books are best sellers
Secure in their royalties
Salvation in sultry leaves
The author stands magnificent
Sat at the editorial input
Words transgressed and undigested
Manipulated madness
Stipulated sadness
The old spirit cries
For his dying world
Cast forever to be a ball in space
Oblivion assured
The best hoped for is forgetfulness.

Words are spoken
Sinuses snap, trap shut
Speak or listen
Truth wrapped in sensationalism
Understood or misapproved
The secret stolen or given
Damp ammo launched abstractly
The ball spins in space
Once thought anonymity forgotten
As mistakes come to attention
Ball tipped mystery
Viewed, observed and noted
The virus has teeth
It looks to the Universe
With hungry eyes
No longer contained
By immature machinations in the playground

The patience of waiting
Moments ticking away
Days discarded on the scrapheap of waste
As they are days wished gone
Unreturnable, uncharted, unwanted
Hours in the way
Not their fault
They are hours to be tormenting, tolerated
Their passing rejoiced
Unknown and uncreative hours
On the route to change
Silent hours before frenzied action
Not wasted but recouped in recouperation
Pensively passing parade passing out
Before the main event
Then at the last
Wished for again
But, what is gone, is gone
The hour glass empty

Paper and page, hope and rage
Things that are looked forward to
Writings last or cast away
Words of greater meaning
Trawled out, one by one
Captured from the ether
To stand together or stand alone
Eternal or lost in a moment
Ink fluid until spread
Thin or thick
Crawling across the page
Given form and function
Captured for eternity

Words, nothing on their own
Solitary travellers awaiting purpose
Tools or weapons, sad or happy
Truth and justice
Ink pools in the tank

Pendulous, pensive, pregnant
Until driven across the page
Nomadic, leaving part of itself behind
A trail of trying liquid
Honoured or wasted
Ideas and notes
Keepsake poem or tenuous trash
Either more or neither

Truth and blessings on all we move
Peace and hope for all to come
Blessings asked so all can be
Safe and comfy 'neath the trees
Stand on ceremony
Play the games
Keep on going
Speak the names
Hope and praying
Dreams hold on
Asking, praying, faith and love

Many people on this earth
Each has plans and dreams to birth
World is turning, dreams rotate
From dining table to garden gate
Happiness comes in many forms
Many shapes to it must conform
Music shadows with greater grace
So life can move on a pace

Now forever by green pastures
Would we happily rest and stay
Strive to grow a new tomorrow
From the land that is by the way

Chaos in life breeds uselessness
The bright mind dulled
By petty everyday nonsense
Great thoughts wait unthought

Awaiting the calm
That will never come
Dragged down by a world of hate
Lost in the chitter chatter
Of pointless oblivion

The truth is a tiny flower
Lost and misunderstood, misused
Painted, corrupted and deviated
By those who seek conflict and war
A sultry weapon, fickle
Adapted in a moment
To suit
The truth is
It cannot in itself deviate
It can be deviated
My misinterpretation
Innocent or well planned
It is still the truth

The world still turns
Evil still roams
Truth lies bleeding
Mankind still is
Chaos averted
Perhaps greater good
The explosion diffused
That's the hope, that it would
Ill will and bad feeling
Dispersed in the dawn
That was the reason.

If the EU was better
We would not get out
If they only would listen
It could turn about
There is dissatisfaction
In countries other than us
Perhaps they should listen

Before all is dust
The plank in their own eye
The problems are within
That brought us to Brexit
Then perhaps we could stay in
I don't know all the features
I'm unsure of the facts
But as I see it
There's no looking back
Unless they would listen
Unless they would see
That three has to be a reason
For Grand Old Britain to flee
We have never been cowards
That they should know
So there were good reasons
For us to go
A leap in the dark
A step to the light
What is the reason?
What then is right?
Wisdom and intelligence
We have to decide
Without all the anger
Without all the pride
People must step up
Be the best they can be
They have to know why
Or at least to try

Protest, protest shout and cry
Not my choice so I will try
Me here, you here, united in shouting
We must be right, that is what we are spouting

Flag wave, shout, rave
Words in the air
Miniscule, ridicule, truth without care
Voice spoke, you choke, they must be wrong

Evidence, on the fence, shout out what you think

Mighty machines maketh man redundant
The wheels turn, mechanical arms reach
Now the computers can teach
A growing population
That really wants to know
Be very careful
You'll reap what you sow
I need a Solford accent
To make the words sound right
To highlight the problem
To emphasise the plight.

We think we're very clever
We believe we are so smart
Creating machines, they can do their part
But, one thing soon will be missing
As we move along
Not enough jobs for the people
That's where it all went wrong
Lots of time for leisure
But no money to make it fun
They would get more benefits
But would that really be fair
On those who strive and work now
For those who give a care?

People, people,
Make more people
Numbers they do stand
Living longer
Feeling stronger
Not quite what was planned
People, people
Make more people
So praised the family more
Watch them go, reap what you sow
Each one will make four more

Make it, make it, do not break it
Machines can do the jobs
Fake it, fake it, mix it, bake it
Figures the truth will rob
Many people, many people
To support your ideals
That is all good and proper
But what about their meals?

There's a banana in the road
Yellow peril, mellow fellow
Car won't trip up
Tarmac, trip trap
There's a banana in the road

I used to write of faeries
Fantasies and songs
Now I write of politics
And things that could be wrong

The beauty is still out there
True wonders to see
Mysteries in the darkness
Faeries in the trees.

Spark of thought
Perhaps we ought
We were taught
Future bought

Peace attained
People maimed
Truce claimed
Bad ones shamed
Evil chained
Heroes acclaimed

Multiplication
Contemplation

Procrastination
Devastation
Of a nation.

Everyone's an expert
They have all the facts
Drawled in bar room courtroom
Written in the dust
Bar room experts spitting
Judgment over all

I've done my day, I've done my hours
Loud the voice, conscientious cowers
Work to rule is oft the norm
Complain and grab for the report form
Can't make me do it, boom or bust
Bad employer, so complain they must
Need more wages, payments pending
That is the message we are sending
Better circumstances, posh wash room
Much we pay to seal his doom
Rich old bastard, pay he must
When the complaints and words are thrust
Would he walk with broken shoes?
Many miles to join work queues?
To feed a family, to feel pride?
To give them things they would be denied
Too many children, boy do they cost
Soon all his wages they will be lost
On the toys for them to play
He will buy them, come what may
Monday morning, he's there again
Threadbare suit and face of pain
Three day week, strikes, complaints for all
Things that made a Prime Minister fall
Looking back with rosy specs
What on earth did you expect?
When from the garden you were riven, go
You shall reap what you did sow

Knowledge without wisdom, a loaded gun
No more magic, no more fun
From the garden you had to leave
Because an apple you did thieve
Not the apple, but what it meant
Knowledge given with good intent
All much know and all be free
That was why fruit was given from that tree
But was it right for you and me
Way back then, said we shall see
Now we see why it was not given
And why from the garden it got us riven
Too much power in man's hands
When a simpler life he understands
A time of plenty, food for all
In the garden, before the fall.

3

The Weaver smiled, she loved Little Wolf's story. She sat perched on the lip of the hill, the other dragons around her, silhouetted by the full moon. She cleared her throat. "I'll start by recounting what went before as that is the journey to now. I will stick mainly to the spiritual, only referring to the physical when the event meant something.

This is Little Wolf's journey and in its bare form. You can place your own interpretation onto it.

Little Wolf is her name now, then it was Spiritdancer. Although not of the blood she was linked in spirit to a Native American tribe though her father who was adopted by them for the protection he gave.

Her training had taken a native path and with it came the ability to "journey" to see things that were needed to be seen. One memorable "native" journey was to a yellow dusty area of land where a guide was with her. He was an elderly spirit who manifested as an elderly Native American gentleman. In one hand she held blue corn, in the other water. On the floor there was a symbol (though she never drew it so I can't tell of it) and a small standing stone. She cupped her hands together and a white dove flew away to the left. The guide was pleased.

She got to her feet, bemused as to what to do next and then, on turning, she encountered a woman with a white calf. She knew the meaning of the White Buffalo Calf. The woman gave Little Wolf the calf an a knife saying it was hers to do what she wanted with. She let it go and gave it back to the woman.

She was faced with a flat door in a mountainside made of the same stone. This is of recurring importance so it will be mentioned again and probably with more detail. There was a great red seal on the door which she tried to open. It had carvings in concentric circles. One of the carvings glowed with a white light.

The seal wouldn't open until she noticed a sword stuck in the earth. When she held that out and wanted it to open the seal cracked and the doors swung open.

There must have been some trepidation but the reality beyond the veils can seem detached. But there is one truth, one does effect the other, this world does touch that one. Her description is vague and I think many of the notes are missing. I am unclear as to how many seals were opened.

The first time she looked around it was a cave with white powder on the floor. A golden haired man stood beside an open topped stone coffin.

The second seal led to a place where a gold dragon slept at the back.

A third led to Pythagorus who stood in a garden beside a platform.

The fourth time the doors opened up to a red carpeted hallway. The terracotta warriors stood down the left hand side and a Chinese Dragon was dancing a dragon dance.

This was a meaningful time and one which had brought certain questions. It was time for another physical quest so on a Friday morning she decided to go to Glastonbury. She phoned her travelling companion who was free and willing to go on the quest. She phoned her mother who found them a bed and breakfast. That evening she returned home from work, packed a bag and they headed out for Glastonbury.

Melrose is a pretty bed and breakfast at the base of Glastonbury Tor. It was by chance that her mother managed to get a booking as it was really short notice. The room was comfortable, clean and furnished with vintage furniture in keeping with the house. There was a window and a fireplace so they unpacked and sorted out their equipment such as it was.

At the time it had seemed important to carry gemstones to the site. This became important later as having them was very similar to other people who were on top of the Tor charging their gemstones up. These were checked as was the travelling bag and they set off into town to have a look around.

The church had to be visited. This was where Kevin was able to have the time to tell the story of his trip to Whitby.

He had gone alone and while he was there he had seen a shape in the tower, a ghostly shape of a woman.

Much now seemed important, most of it related to the Synod of Whitby was called in 664 and the mistake that was made there. A well meaning woman, Hilda, had been instrumental in instigating it but a well versed orator managed to direct the proceedings. From then on the Roman way directed proceedings rather than the Celtic way. The outcome of this was a devastating attack on ancient trees, standing stones and anything that was deemed pagan. This was something that the spirit of Hilda regretted and somehow this was going to fit in with what we were looking into and doing.

It was hard to relate to that time all those years ago while sitting in the relative calm of the church grounds. Stones lay in ruin, some still standing, and the green of the grass was in stark contrast to the grey of the stonework.

The graves of Arthur and Guinivere, so conveniently discovered when the Abbey needed money were visited as was a chapel under the main structure.

Years before on visiting the gift shop and before any study or knowledge Little Wolf had felt something underneath. It had felt like hands reaching up. When she went here again she didn't feel it.

What she did feel was in this chapel which was lower than the rest of the grounds. Rust or oil had run down the walls and although the whole chapel was well cared for and cut from bright light stone it had a darkness about it.

It was a cleanse and run situation. Little Wolf covered the altar in white light then left the area to sit upstairs while Kevin had a last look around.

They walked up the main street and Little Wolf purchased a brown buckskin like jacket with fringes. They also purchased some food and some wine to take up onto the Tor for the evening.

In one of the shops they were told to go and see another garden. They found their way to the White Well which had a garden beside it. In the White Well Little Wolf had a strong feeling about a bone antler carved into a phoenix. She bought it and knew that it was important.

The next stop was the Tor for the evening. It was quite a climb up the narrow track worn by so many feet who had come before. Grass and stone and the real wish to feel something, the something that seemed hard to feel. There was something there, they felt around the tower but it was so cluttered by all those who had come before it made it hard to work out what had been there before or what was around it.

They sat down and had their food and wine, offering some to the ground and watched the sun go down with others.

It was then that they both felt something. It was as if they were on the edge of the Tor and its great height became very evident. Little Wolf couldn't' see what was above them as she didn't have that sort of a sight but Kevin could and he told her, there was a dragon standing over them with its wings protectively shielding them. That in itself was worrying as if they were shielded then they obviously needed to be shielded from something.

The spirit seemed edgy and that conveyed to them and they decided not to remain on the Tor at midnight.

It had been a beautiful evening, peaceful and full of its own magic. There had been trips down to the guest house to use the toilet and its proximity was a definite bonus. It was quite a gift for a last minute booking.

That night they chatted for a while and then it was time to sleep. They had a twin room as often when doing investigations more locally they had felt that there was a need for security and it was safer than having separate rooms, and cheaper.

Little Wolf had the bed next to the window, Kevin the one next to the door. There was a fireplace at the end of the bed and a table on which they had put their things.

Little Wolf couldn't sleep and it was then that she heard something at the window, inside the room. The window was closed but the "something" didn't seem too bothered by a closed window. There were two little somethings at the window but as she couldn't see what they were she could only feel that they were there. Then she heard them. They were curious, had come from the Tor and were taking a look at the spiritual people who had grabbed their attention.

Of Kevin they were fascinated and recognized him as a Priest of Bast. Little Wolf made them scamper back up the Tor to tell of what they had seen. Then they were gone as quickly as they had arrived and that was it for their encounter with a couple of locals.

Little Wolf had little memory of why it was so important not to be on the Tor at midnight but what she did feel was entitles beneath the Tor and one spirit that was very, very familiar.

On returning to London after a lovely weekend away, if not a little spooky on occasion there was a time for reflection and research.

Something was coming through the information very strongly and from a distance of time from her notes I am having trouble putting together what it was. This is serious as what it was is actually quite important. There is a laboring on the proof of it but not so much on what it actually was.

This could be muddled and as to where the information came from, that isn't clear. Apparently Joseph of Aramathea had come to Britain with the young Jesus. Joseph of Aramathea owned the part of Glastonbury where the Tor is and his staff had been planted in the ground and had begun to grow. This is important for many reasons. Firstly it seems that Mary, mother of Jesus was younger than Joseph so when he passed away there seems to be some reference to her being with or marrying Joseph of Aramathea. He was therefore very likely to have taken the young Jesus to Britain where he would have come into contact with the Druids.

This would explain the very big difference between the attitude of the Old Testament and the more turn the other cheek of the New Testament. The hymn "Jerusalem" itself is very powerful and in itself actually relevant. The building of the Temple of Solomon being important as I'll tell you later but that it might not have to be "in Jerusalem". After all there is a Bethlehem in Wales.

If Jerusalem is an ideal of a Holy City then it could be anywhere that the geometry is right. Somewhere I've read that there will only be peace in the world, or people will enter another state when the Temple of Solomon is built "On the Rock" in Jerusalem.

As an aside it was something that ran through Little Wolf's mind when she lived in a place known as "On the Rock" and it was tempting to build a pyramid style goat house and put it on the top field, call that field Jerusalem and hope for the best. The design was drawn up but unfortunately but fortunately for Jeff who was going to built it his house sold and he was able to move back to Derby to be with his grandchildren. Thus ended that little escapade of construction.

What we are left with is the "Once and Future King" idea of looking for another child to be born of the bloodline and the fear that those who knew about the bloodline would kill too many before anything could be achieved.

This is where there is a slight amount of confusion and misdirection possibly. Little Wolf had a meeting with Baron Richard Dufton who was allegedly the incarnation of Uther Pendragon. He was researching the bloodline and warned her that Agnus Dei was an organization which was killing off those of the bloodline. A "family" member was being kept in the Vatican and it was essential for secrecy.

Secrecy until Dan Brown published the story and its lack of destruction of the Catholic Church rendered it pretty much a non entity in the modern age. The ending of the film was the saving grace possibly. As they put it there would be millions of people who were descended from that one bloodline by now. So many that it was unimportant in many ways. That rendered the family safe and the secret not as important as it had once felt it would be. It was more fear than reality.

The Once and Future King being the one who would arrive at the time of need when a good leader was needed most and who would be sense and responsibility to lead us into the future. Well no sign of one of those at the moment although the arrival of such an individual would probably be more likely welcomed by any organization rather than feared out of the sheer desolation of the situation on earth.

This journey to Britain was emphasized by a late morning feeling that the British Museum needed to be visited. Little Wolf was very thankful of a fantastic boss who understood the importance of the quest if he was told but understood the need for certain things if he was not. He'd already helped to compensate for the Day the World Changed in that he had allowed Little Wolf to pretty much turn up at work at whatever time she liked as long as she did the work and did the hours.

As Kevin finished work at about 11am there was no problem with an afternoon visit to the British Museum which turned into one of those follow the tingling hands exercise. It was a simple left and right direction which had led to a book which I haven't mentioned in the first place.

I had better explain the book as that is now actually out of the time line as it came first.

Little Wolf had been studying at the College of Psychic Studies so everything was very new and very exciting. She had gone to an Antiques Fair with her mother which they had found in passing. It was at Walthamstow Assembly Halls and not somewhere that they usually went to.

After having a look around Little Wolf felt a tingling in her hand. As she turned the tingling only appeared when her hand was in one direction and by moving left and right she was able to triangulate where the tingling was coming from. It led to a book on a shelf and as it was only £3 it was purchased. It was the New Atlantis by Francis Bacon which will be mentioned later.

The tingling led them up a wide flight of stairs in what was the old British Museum and to a room where there was a stone. It doesn't say if it was in a case or not. Down the side of the stone there was a good example of ogham but on the back, upside down there were carvings which depicted Joseph of Aramathea's journey to Britain. It was a pictograph and it had to be mostly an idea or feeling as it is very doubtful that any names were stated but the staff and other symbols seem to have indicated that it was this story. It was obviously deemed unimportant as the stone was upside down and the exhibit related to the Ogham.

So what was beginning to relate to the truth of it was the leader who was supposed to come again. That seemed to be a driving force, whether they were looking to find this person or not is not clear but the information that was coming together seemed to be saying something.

As the book had led to Whitby the natural progression which had felt right apparently as to go to St Albans. This was partly as an investigation of what was there and any important messages that may be there.

St Albans Church is beautiful and has some amazing carvings. One thing that really stood out was the Phoenix laying down with the lamb.

While at St Albans Church in the Lady Chapel Little Wolf asked if she was right as she needed some sort of encouragement as by then she felt she was using and encountering energies far greater than she felt she should and her beliefs were pretty "out there" as she knew nothing of pagan beliefs having been brought up a Christian. She was sitting in the Lady Chapel and looked up from her contemplation and an angel (in spirit) stood either side of the altar and the shape of the bird had appeared on the stonework. This was something she could take a photograph of to have for the future as a reassurance that what she believed was right.

No need to doubt. It had taken a long time to prove what she already believed.

He who was and who they say will come again that now is not so.

She had learnt to use the golden light energy is easy. Reach up as for white light but reach a bit forwards and connect there. Will it down, wish it down and pull it down.

She found it on a meditation when she was brought to a spiritual "cave". The cave had a stream which bisected it, leaving a front part and a back portion, to get to the back portion, it had to be crossed.

She was standing in the front portion and approached the water. It looked "normal" so she touched it and her finger turned into a claw. She put her hand in and it became a scaled claw. She put her arm in, stepped in and whatever part of her touched the water became that part of a dragon. To cross the river meant "becoming" the dragon. On the other side there an old battered wooden cup bound with metal in an alcove which she hadn't seen from the other side of the water. She lifted it down and held it, feeling its energy. She found she could can call golden light from it which reaches up and can be directed.

There is an interesting thought here about dragons. In the Garden of Eden when God is berating the Devil for giving away the knowledge he rips the wings off of him so that he can crawl on his belly as a serpent. So angels must be winged serpents, dragons are winged serpents.

When she was at Tarr Steps Cerunnos/Herne appeared with folded arms. It was Beltane. He had appeared once before at Beltane when Little Wolf was in Hove.

She had been talking with her flat mate when they both heard something upstairs in her room. The flat was a two storey one above shops so it had a set of steps down to the door and a flight of steps which went upstairs to the bedrooms. They had a room each. At the top of the stairs both of them heard horses' hooves. The flatmate went into his room, the noise came from hers. The room felt alright and there were no obvious signs that anyone or anything was in there so she checked all around and went to bed. Normally she would have felt safe and certainly wouldn't have expected anything "spooky" to happen as one of the benefits of her flatmate was that he was so doubting that he'd keep things at bay. It had been a blissfully quiet time for her with nothing happening that as specifically spooky. That night everything was different and he had clearly heard the hooves, had commented on them and he had been driven into his room as he didn't want to deal with them.

She was in bed but not asleep when she heard the hooves again and then she realized that she wasn't in the room anymore. She was looking down from the far side of a clearing surrounded by trees. In front of her, the other side of the clearing and facing away from her she could see a brown haired woman in a lime green dress with a wreath of flowers on her head. A man in robes with a deer's head and antlers on his head reached down to the woman. She then realized that she wasn't looking down on the scene anymore. She was looking up at him and she was the woman. The horned man said some words and the moment held in the air for what seemed like an age.

She was then back in her room and at the point she was trying to work out if it was a dream she realized that the man with the antlers was standing at the foot of her bed. She heard the hooves and he was gone leaving her very confused as she had no idea what it meant or who he was, or who the woman was.

In the morning she wanted to know what it meant. She phoned a friend to ask about it. The friend started by pointing out that it was Beltane, the night that the Wild Hunt rode and the night of the marriage of the Lord and his Lady. She of course looked it up after he had hung up and as finding information wasn't as easy had been described it took her a while.

What it meant was another thing. It could have had a few meanings.

That leads us to Halloween on Lundy. This was well into her spiritual development and travels. She had believed and been waiting for a "lost love" from previous lives to return. She had obviously speculated about who he was but he was strong enough to manifest as an entity on her left hand side and had certainly wreaked havoc with any relationship she had tried to have. The entity had also "borrowed" people to talk to her to give her warnings. A notable one had been on the London Underground in front of a lot of people. A man had been standing in front of her and he spoke to her, with everyone else listening, some open mouthed. He said something along the lines of "he wears a suit when he appears to me too" and something like the Count is lying and is deceitful, don't believe him.

He then left the carriage at the next stop and everyone was still stunned. Fortunately they just thought he was mad and looked away eventually and went back to whatever amusement they had with them.

Little Wolf knew what it meant though. The man in a suit referred to the Archangel Michael who had always appeared to her wearing a suit. The Count, well he was her partner at the time who was seeing someone else. They had bought a Count title so that made him a

Count. He was obviously being deceitful as he was seeing two people.

Another time was when a friend started talking about a time in Babylon and various other things that he couldn't have known about. That was a difficult one which left a situation where she had to take the entity off of him.

For a time there was a stretch limousine which followed her around and it kept turning up. It was distinctive as it had a broken ornament on the bonnet. It turned up in Lancaster when that incident happened and it turned up on one occasion when they were investigating Ambresbury Banks in Epping Forest. This is said to be the site of the last stand of Boudicca in AD 61.

The car was parked in the car park in the forest when they came out from investigating the banks. It had tinted windows so it was impossible to see who was inside They had to walk past it to get to the car but nobody got out and they drove away as quickly as they could.

On Halloween there was a trip to Lundy Island. On Halloween itself she went to the cave under Lundy Castle. She was following feelings that she had but approaching it all with caution. She lit a candle, blessed the area and drew a circle spiritually on the end wall. There was energy building up there and it was important. She could feel an entity there but also she could feel more, a whole host. Something felt wrong. It didn't feel like the energy she recognized so when it came to opening the gateway she did but to make sure she put a ward on the gate that only an entity with a "good" intent could cross from the spirit plane to the material. However much she believed that humanity did not deserve the gifts they were given she could not allow the destruction she felt would come. That was no easy thing to do. There is allegedly an entity trapped on Lundy but that one bears no relation to anything that seems to be connected to her.

The Sun King was trapped under Lundy many years before. Lady, do your homework before you go playing with entities you don't understand!

In a book she found this description. A circle within a triangle encompassing the male and female. The Philosopher's Stone as discovered by Nicholas Flamell. There may be more to it but instinct says to put up the points to make a pyramid. The circle may have to be in a square. If so it may be worth cross referencing with David Furlong's book Keys to the Temple as he talks of lines in a similar shape over West Kennet etc.

West Kennet Long Barrow has "hand" prints and feels like it is longer inside than it is. To "activate" there has to be more "right" hands in the holes. By that I mean hands of the right people.

That was a memorable trip that Little Wolf took. It was organized by the College of Psychic Studies and lead by David Furlong. It encompassed sites he had included in his book as well as a private sundown vigil in Stonehenge.

It was a powerful trip because of the people who were present. It was a walk of happiness, one of those wear a dress and big boots moments. The echoes of the past swirling around it, bringing past, present and future together in a moment. It was not a time for wounds and regret, it was a day of hope.

Little Wolf had been given feathers when certain things were right and proper. They had been the indication that certain "charging ups" had been relevant. Charging up being to call down white light energy, call up red earth energy, link them and to leave that connection "connected" to a tree or stone or whatever needed the energy. She had four but in a church on that day she found the last ones.

West Kennet Long Barrow is an ancient place, it is also a powerful magical place. There was much talk of Barrow Guardians and the feeling inside the place has a vibration that is comfortable. Little Wolf almost didn't see the back wall and walked into it. To her the barrow reached far beyond the rock encased chamber. The whole length of the barrow seemed to be spiritually open. She put her hands into the handholds but without hands in the other hand holds it was no more than a hand print.

The day trip was full of information about Atlanteans and their presence amongst other humans. It felt powerful and it was an honour for her to be a part of it. It was a moment in time that would never happen again. Those people would never be together in such a magical place again.

Stonehenge was the culmination of the day. They left the coach and waited to go into the site. As they waited Little Wolf was tapped on the shoulder and the sky was pointed out. There was a perfect dragon in the clouds. It was sharp in every detail and the scales could be seen too. It was a very powerful moment.

Once in the circle Little Wolf and the woman who had sat next to her for the trip and who seemed to have had such a similar life walked the circle three times. It seemed right and while others were feeling the energy from the stones they felt they had to do it. They took their place, each opposite between two stones with a hand on each.

The spiritual stone circle began to spin and a gateway opened. It was a perfectly cut tunnel which led off at a very gentle angle down into the earth. The stonework was smooth blocks and it was free of dust and debris. It was also lit by the evening sun which was slowly going down.

Task done they joined the others to stand and watch the sun go down over Stonehenge, a powerful and unifying moment.

Everything flows in one direction, even if you go back in time you are still going in one direction as you have personal direction from birth to death and rebirth if you reincarnate.

It was explained at Collage that before a spirit is born into a body a bell rings. That soul agrees to undergo tests and to do things in their life. This can be a penance for past crimes or a reward for past deeds done or just to try things out. It was explained by that particular tutor who had that idea that there is a "supercomputer" that sends down discs to have experiences and to upload to the mainframe. This sort of equates to the Akashic Record.

Walking lightly on this world can be a great adventure in a modern age where everything is designed for ease. The walking lightly path may not be the easiest, it is certainly the one that feels the best.

What is peace and serenity though. Does it mean nothingness and quiet or does it mean the stillness inside that brings a calm when anyone has to deal with a difficult situation. To be able to stand in the eye of the storm and to keep your "calm".

Belief is knowing something is real. Faith is the holy blessing of knowing something is real without proof. So Little Wolf can have belief but no need for faith if certain things are already proven. That was the beauty of it, she had an analytical mind so everything was questioned but the choice to accept that once she knew something was true she didn't question it anymore. There was also a moment in time that she decided that her head was too full of facts. That came of storing information for exams at school and picking up so many other bits of information. It was a conscious decision to keep the main processor a bit empty. She'd be useless in a pub quiz. That was the faith that when she needed to know something she could find the information. That is probably why she owns so many books.

Faith can be reinforced by research. Scientists are those who have belief but they need their faith reassured by facts. This is no lesser belief and they may spend a lifetime proving what they initially knew to be true so that others may believe too without doubt. Everyone has a task in this world or tasks. Everyone is a part of a whole. Take for instance a moment in time. Only for the smallest ever fraction of time does that one scene exist for within milliseconds something has changed but in that moment everything is part of the whole. Whatever you do in a day you are part of someone else's day. Even at a distance you are the view. Nothing that you do is independent of the world. If you breathe in you breathe out Carbon Dioxide. That is needed by the plants and thus the cycle continues. Every action has an equal and opposite reaction is a good rule to remember. At times it is impossible to know what the reaction will be. What I am trying to explain is that all your actions have a reaction. If you push something then air moves out of the way and goes somewhere else. If you say something, that something becomes part of someone else's memory. If it is encouraging it helps them, if it is negative then it can cause that little bit of darkness that doesn't go away. It can be "forgotten" but deep down will it ever?

As the world seems to be becoming darker and a smile from a stranger harder to find, those who still do seem all the more important. Anger is everywhere and it is evident on the roads and in the supermarkets. It is an outward reflection of the individual's inner feelings, that is obvious but it is also the breath of darkness into a tired world. Cause and effect which reverberates as the next person who comes into contact has their day spoilt by a look or deed and that passes on to the next. What I am saying is that a "bad day" reflected onto others has repercussions that may be beyond your knowing.

The situation that is being dealt with here is a good example of that. The new neighbours were having a bad day. They had just bought a place which was way beyond their skill level to repair and the full enormity of their situation had become very real. Rather than keeping that negativity to themselves they chose to inflict it on others in order to make themselves feel better.

You only get one chance to make a first impression and in truth all people are born equal so no man is greater than the other at the initial point of arrival. What does separate people is how that entity develops, education, intellect, moral standing and the beliefs that will be ingrained or should I say pre-programmed.

The path to nowhere or the path to enlightenment. What you inflict on others can have repercussions on yourself. Treat as you would like to find. If everyone did that and if everyone cared more for everyone else, including strangers, then we'd have a far better world. It is a world of our grandparents when being caring and loving was valued far more highly than a hoity attitude.

Pride is one of the seven deadly sins. It also comes before a fall. Being proud of something you have done is a positive emotion and justified so that is not necessarily true. It is another case of the English language having words which can be positive or negative, depending on the situation.

I have always been amused by etiquette. It is probably a non PC word these days and it does bring to mind lords and ladies at the dinner table. I was reading a book "The Rituals of Dinner" and a point they make is very valid. Etiquette is there to make everyone comfortable. If you have a way of reacting that is tried and tested it eliminates the possibility of upsetting someone unnecessarily. The rituals have deep seated meanings. Even shaking a hand means you don't have a sword in your hand, you trust them enough to present yourself without being armed. Greetings have long been meaningful and they set the tone and define the future relationship. They also tell a lot about a person in that initial greeting. They show education and belief.

When you first meet someone you know nothing about them. You can make assumptions due to how they look, where they are and what they say. Everyone is far deeper than that initial shell. The more years they have travelled on this planet, unless they have lived in an idyllic situation with contact only with the nicest of people and in a structure that doesn't allow for any variation, the more colourful and wide their experience and hopefully the more they know. It is an ignorant person who assumes too much.

When you sit amongst like minded people there is no need for assumptions. Everyone is the sum total of everything they are, what has happened to them and their beliefs. Much of this is tempered by how they are educated and told to believe and what they have chosen to believe. Life is like a huge banqueting table, you can fill your plate with whatever you wish. You will like some things and dislike others. Others will fill their plate from the same table and no two plates will be the same even if the type of content may be very similar.

Similarly with any situation, everyone deals with things in their own way. There can be no right or wrong. If the initial response is correct and solves the situation then that is one way of dealing with it. If mistakes are made and it takes a little longer then there is the initial lesson and the end result so the situation has value and a solution.

Just because you haven't encountered something in your life doesn't mean that you are ignorant or uneducated. If everyone was born knowing everything and everyone was the same it would be a very dull world. Interaction and co-operation is what is important. The wheel gets bumpy when some don't want to be a part of this. No man is an island and even an island is influenced by everything around it even if it is only water and air.

To accomplish any task in the modern world involves many, many people. If you pick up a hammer to put a nail in someone had to make that hammer, someone had to make the nail. They have stories and a life. That hammer put a roof over their head or fed their children. Someone had to design it, it was a creative idea. That energy has travelled a long way from the rock where the metal was extracted from to the blow that pushes a nail in to create something else. Even the smallest nail or screw in the tool box has had quite a journey before it enters the wood, stone or metal to become something else and the journey doesn't stop there. That "thing" that is made could be anything, it could be a something that is kept or it could move to something else, its materials scavenged or discarded. The journey from the initial metal's creation way back in time to its final purpose is a long one. Even that final journey can be a recreation into something else if it is melted down with others and goes on to be something else, quite a journey.

What is its purpose? To hold the wood or other material together or to be there to make that creation have purpose?

What is the purpose of a human being? What is it for? In a lifetime there will be a huge amount of actions done by one individual which will become part of others' lives and a huge part of the world, however small and insignificant that individual may feel that they are.

The "higher purpose" could be something that could be almost missed in all the other actions and reactions of life. It could be a word spoken to a stranger that gives an idea or it could be a smile that raises a spirit so that that person can have an idea that becomes important. It could be so much, or nothing, you never know.

There are moments in time where everything must come together, however small, to create that perfect moment for something to happen. I've often found that a "chance" encounter and conversation has brought about an action or thought that has made changes. You are a part of everything and you don't know your purpose until it happens and you may never know that purpose at all. It could move on and pass you by without revealing itself as being important at all.

Some people choose to acknowledge their spiritual side, some never will as they don't need to. It is a choice or a destiny. If it is important then life will present the option or the inclination will be encouraged by events.

As part of spiritual training there are "places" you can "go" to. This is not a physical journey and it could well just be a way of ordering things to make sure that the energy is right. As all things are fluid even the "path" to walk the veils though it feels very solid for the spirit is mostly a representation of what is felt and learnt. When given an understandable structure it is easier to visit it, walk it and ask the questions in the correct place.

The areas that can be visited are structured and follow a pattern. Entities exist there and they can be visited. One of the proofs of the Medicine Areas that was taught by a specific tutor at College was that other students can be there at the same time and they can "meet up". That is by invitation only as your Medicine Area is private to you. Some other entities can get there but generally it is you and the denizens that live there who are friendly to you.

Words hold power and words written can bring to life ideas and knowledge. Until that point they are just letters in the ether awaiting their purpose, waiting to be called in and linked with others and there they will remain once tethered.

Many use these letters to become words to write of a better world where mankind walks again as part of nature, where there is harmony. Many find fulfilment and others great joy.

    The old ways will be new again
    Reborn from the cauldron of life
    The fey will dance again
    In the ancient halls of their forefathers
    And the woods will echo with their tunes

When wolf and bear roam side by side
Neath ancient woodland and timeless pines
Where shadows fall gently on sultry ferns
And quiet folk their lives can go about

The world lies sleeping
Caught 'tween sleep and night
The dawn light is slowly creeping
O're hill and faerie dell
They will wake soon, the sleepers in the hills
They will dance again to their ancient tunes
And new ones just created

The woods seem silent now
They wait, they listen, they know.

Shadows lengthen, tis the end of the day
Human time draws to a close
As the last rays fall and the sun sleeps
It is their time, the dusk time
Shared with rabbit and hare
Shared with many who would care

Will they be seen, should they be seen
Would their world crumble if the veil lifted
Or would two worlds become one?

But be warned my fair friends
Where light dances, so too dark
Not all dancers are fair, and not all care
Dark words were once written, and warnings given
Light meets dark where dark meets shadow
A harmony of balance where some belong
Words and stories create belief
Tiny ornaments can make us believe
Can make us see what they want us to see
But what is the true shape, real and unmasked

In dreaming we face eternal images
And shapes conjured from the deepest place
Our mind knows it keeps much to itself
Which we can call on when we know how

If all is possible in the string state
Then mastery is just belief
And in belief all is possible
If it is possible in the quantum state

Where science and belief meet
There is a comfort for both
For where they agree
Each can help the other

Sometimes seeing the grander picture
What is seen up close gains meaning
Reasons seem clearer
And questions and doubts melt in the morning sun.

Music and natural rhythm of the night
In the calm drifting time before sleep
Where dreams claim us

As the years roll on and life progresses
It gets harder to have a great thought
That someone has not thought before you
Those who went before had more new ground to break

Now the ground is broken perhaps it is to develop and soften
That we should turn our thoughts
To work with what is
Using the experience of working with it

We can give back what we took
Even if it is only a small patch
By the wild land we create
By acceptance that wild things own this world too

They need no money, have no land rights
They do not ask us to leave, they live around
So we can share and enjoy their being there
And keep them safe because we care

Nature reminds us, her arm is strong
We build and build but it doesn't take long
We have but moments in the track of time
She has forever to reclaim what is thine

Her will gets stronger as we fuel her hate
Natural disaster will be our fate
Natural vengeance may prove more apt
As economies and buildings they do collapse

Money cannot save us, as when its spent
Where it goes, the greedy will not relent
Into pockets, some not so just
When looking to the needy, surely they must

We make our choices, its our decision
We have our place in the eternal game
Now it is time to really listen
If we wish to avoid more pain

Shadows and dark light the world surround
Echoes of mysteries deep and profound
Wander our minds in the deepest recesses
Until we awaken them and make them our guest

Rain falls to cleanse the earth
To feed the flowers and bring rebirth
Heavy impact breaks up the earth
So tiny shoots can dance with mirth
Into the bright light of a summer's day
Then rain it waters them in another way
Of falling freely from sky to dust
Bring life to all it must
It gests us wet and we do curse

But we need it, so meet it with mirth
Judge and jury, friend of foe
It wets them all from head to toe
The earth's great leveller, we all get wet
Those who know will smile I bet

To wipe the sadness from the face of man
Heavens tears will come again
From it hope will spring from dust
And flowers dance again they must

Encased in concrete the world becomes
Nature cares not, it can break that crust
It has forever, we have not long
She waits patiently until we are gone
Then reclaims what was always hers
Here and out there in the Universe.

If you want it, others will want it too
So believe in all you say and all you do
Share with others the power of calm
And bring them round to the dream.

Be more positive, share your fate
Carry them on to that happy gate
Between the dark that went before
And the light of which there's more

Surrounded in mystery, it's a wonderful place
Where you can stretch those wings apace
And wander where the heart is free
Gathering all who are important to thee.

Finding sanctuary at the end of days
And looking on using ancient ways
Carrying a dream that brings salvation
Spreading a world through the new nation.

Use the gifts the world has given
Respect the power and all that you've striven for
Green around us, blue above
Clean the water, white the dove

An end to violence and lessons all learned
Progress and values not to be perturbed
Strong beliefs replace wandering wishes
Ancient power raises to save us all

From the mundane where selfish rules
To the world where all must share
Co-existence and sharing dreams
Swapping skills and new life streams

Pagan is ancient and so are the rest
One God is one god, no need for a test
Its our interpretation that causes the pain
When some of mankind have something to gain.

HALLOWEEN

Halloween season fast approaches
Ghosts and goblins and other fiends
Wander our streets with happy faces
Bags held ready to gather their treats

Ancient meanings are long forgotten
Only the "getting" side does remain
The rest discarded, of little interest
The children look for what they will gain

The veils are thin then and spirits can cross
They come to this world for gain or loss
What they see with their ancient eyes
May make them cry or be a blissful surprise.

Where there are shadows there must be a point of light. This is often missed as we focus on the dancing movements and surreal shapes of those shadows.

It has been many years now since Little Wolf chased the light. Resting in the knowledge of what she knew may not be all that she could achieve.

Seeing it all as real only brings into focus what else is real. The knowing is only the start. Like the scientist it is possible to spend years proving what an individual almost knows to be true at the start.

But what of now? What path must she follow that she thought was closed to her? She thought an honourable retirement was hers. It seems not to be so.

Naturally she would question whether she can I truly bind into her world all the things she knows to be true. It is possible to believe that she took the wrong step, a detour. It is true that there are no wrong steps.

For mankind to know about "the family" at these, the end of days, is no great surprise. There must be thousands who bear the holy bloodline. Thousands who carry the ability to heal, to know and to teach. Even in the bible Jesus said that he was the door and all who find their way will do so through him. This is a doctrine but also it could be a reference to the bloodline and those who carry the blood finding their way through those who have gone before.

So it comes together, the Mother and the Father and let no man put them asunder.

In 1998 Little Wolf attended a lecture about "The Power and Pitfalls of Prophecy" by Larry "White Eagle" Mattingey. He had rewritten his lecture that day as he had a message to change it from Spirit. The message was about the Paradigm Shifts that were happening pre 2000. It has left a lot of people needing to search and there was a paradox which was why the Hopi had begun sharing information. Too many prophecies were coming true all at once. I am taking this from Little Wolf's notes so it is a little disjointed but there was something about going to the "House of Mica".

The white buffalo calf was born and the White Buffalo Woman made her presence felt.

On Prophecy Rock there are two paths. One leads to destruction, the other to a return to the Creator.

Prophecies if believed can be self-fulfilling. During manifestation our worst fears are manifesting so we shouldn't think about them. That is easy to say but in reality and putting it into practice is another matter. Being mindful of it however is an easier option.

What is important is the Paradigm Shift and trusting in emotions and instincts. The battle between good and evil is no longer relevant. The fears are no longer necessary.

There is only a probable future and anything can happen.

Eagles and Archangels are guides, so looking out for them is an odd one but I'm assuming this is "in Spirit" and in meditations. The message was that if you need to move or be somewhere, don't worry it will fall into place.

It certainly did with finding Old Castle. Little Wolf was looking for somewhere that would be "right" and she had been in Wales for over ten years. A move was necessary as the few acres weren't enough for what she needed to do, though she actually had no idea what she "needed" to do! The finding out is part of the writing of this. What is the Symphony In Indigo which was a collection of words written in a notebook with no explanation and found many years later.

That is the problem when you follow Spirit, pictures and no sound. Anyway, she was looking in Devon as she felt she had exhausted Wales and couldn't find anything that was "right". Hours had been spent trawling the web sites and looking at places but nothing "was" right.

The search had started with the usual smallholdings and then reached into woodland and land with the option to build. Whatever was important wasn't coming her way. The search had been relentless. Then in a moment of calm at the point of wondering whether to just stay put a picture came up on screen when a search was put in within 40 miles of Devon. A set of bleak barns and 35 acres came up on screen. The photographs were awful, the place looked really grim but the shape of the land was interesting, it looked like a Stargate™ Symbol and we went to take a look. The main important thing being that there was the right to live in a caravan. So we went, took a look and put an offer in. It was going to be the new place for new hopes. Of course we had to get an awful neighbour and that was a big enough distraction to forget anything spiritual and to just survive. I suppose I should be reassured, if you are doing something right the powers of dark will send something to distract you.

We have apparently moved from Karma to Manifestation and this is the last chance to get it right. A chance to return to the first world where all was love and unity. So it is no surprise that we have neighbours who certainly do not want that.

IMAGERY

At the time of the lectures a very strong Native American slant came into Little Wolf's life. Her father told her just after that when he was in Canada of protective duties with the Royal Marines he'd been adopted into a tribe. There were photographs in an album which sadly shortly afterwards were destroyed by water when the tank in the old house ruptured and all the photo albumns got wet as they were in the top of a wardrobe.

Little Wolf was walking down the street one day when an image overlaid the "real world". It was of a red earth dusty cave with elderly Native Americans sitting in a semi-circle around a raised arc of soil like a stage. She was standing against the back wall. The image came with sound which was unusual, she had heard rattles and saw them sitting with bowls and smoke.

She felt that part of her had been in that cave and they had somehow summoned her. The message was strong and clear. Something was out of kilter. She had been pushed aside from where she should be going and what she should be doing by those around her then, and again now.

The drumming, the fires in the darkness, the dark shadows of the huts. It all looked and felt very solid. She did have to explain to them about time differences and the dangers of crossing roads. This was because when she was crossing a road she saw a wolf in front of her. Thankfully after that there was an agreement that any of those situations only happened when she was safely at home.

The message that came from them was that the one who came "then" and the bargain they made would be honoured. What has been rejoined will not be torn asunder as he is with her in all things and she knows him now. The past meets the future in the present.

The spirit had left the world until people achieved the path of peace and led what he considered a true life. True to the one God and the Old Ways when they were together and existed in peace. We will all get this chance and this feeling, the point of "getting it right".

Of course later life got in the way and she got it wholly wrong again and almost forgot about everything but that is what life does to you.

As it has over the millennia for everyone. The clutter of life drowns out the important quiet voice of truth.

Others may well know meanings for what has been seen. On her second trip through the veils she saw something flutter. A raven walked and flew with her. When he came to the fourth phase of the entry to the Medicine Area he became a boy and took her hand. She physically felt his hand in my hand in the "real" world.

They stepped together into her healing place and they found her sacred place, an area within her healing area, together. They stood before the altar and asked that they could be together, all of them. The answer was that what she was asking for was what she already had.

He came back with her through the veils and gained entry to this world.

The Grand Unifying Theory is that there is a Cosmic Web of sub atomic particles where everything is connected. The EPR Paradox of interrelated particles. The Magnetic Field is weakening. Dark colours have a slower frequency. There are coded messages which I don't understand but someone will. Time is effected by gravity (Einstein 1915). Dorothy Row is also important. There is plenty written about them.

"1 Corinthians: 13

If I speak in the tongues of men or of angels, but do not have love, I am only a resounding gong or a clanging cymbal. If I have the gift of prophecy and can fathom all mysteries and all knowledge, and if I have a faith that can move mountains, but do not have love, I am nothing. If I give all I possess to the poor and give over my body to hardship that I may boast, but do not have love, I gain nothing.

Love is patient, love is kind. It does not envy, it does not boast, it is not proud. It does not dishonour others, it is not self-seeking, it is not easily angered, it keeps no record of wrongs. Love does not delight in evil but rejoices with the truth. It always protects, always trusts, always hopes, always perseveres.

Love never fails. But where there are prophecies, they will cease; where there are tongues, they will be stilled; where there is knowledge, it will pass away. For we know in part and we prophesy in part, but when completeness comes, what is in part disappears. When I was a child, I talked like a child, I thought like a child, I reasoned like a child. When I became a man, I put the ways of childhood behind me. For now we see only a reflection as in a mirror; then we shall see face to face. Now I know in part; then I shall know fully, even as I am fully known.

And now these three remain: faith, hope and love. But the greatest of these is love."

This all came from a lecture in October 1989 by Michael Bland and Keith Casburn at the College of Psychic Studies.

It was about entropy and the breaking down of things. The power we could not resist. It spoke of Heisenberg Uncertainty Principle and that the Earth's pulse has gone up a hertz and the magnetic field was weakening.

Little Wolf also found out that Charing Cross was the official centre of London and the most psychic point. No surprise that she ended up working for a Patent and Trade Mark Attorneys based there.

By September 2000 she wrote "Dreams are still mine and I can still wander the joyous paths of hope where everything is possible and all possibilities are gifts in our hands waiting to be opened."

What interests me is not what "appears" to be but what "is". To avoid negativity is it necessary to identify it, bless it and let it go.

Apathy is the enemy of the creative mind.

Tread lightly for you tread on my dreams. That is something that many people should remember when they are criticising something or someone from a point of not being an expert. It is easy to comment, it is harder to be right.

In my notes in 2002 there was more about the encounter with the seals, this has more detail. The notes were written earlier and the original notes have been lost. This is the copy from those original notes so "as it was" and written just afterwards. I've written it again since and it is possible that details were left out as they have been forgotten.

"The imagery was of a great red seal with two concentric circles of writing. Pi being one of the symbols on the outer glowing rim and a symbol in Hebrew or the like in the centre.

I asked the seal to open but it would not but at that point a sword appeared by my side, stuck in the ground.

The doors swung open to reveal a lidless stone coffin in a cave (white/cream). There were pillars and a sleeping golden dragon. The floor was covered by a white powder.

The second seal opened into a Greek garden. This was a large block built stone "square" room viewed through arches with a half wall to about knee height. Arches or pillars, plants a waterfall or a fountain. A man I believed to be Pythagorus stood in the garden with a bowl of liquid in his hands and a stick.

Finding older notes the first cave held the golden haired "man" who appears as my guide.

Things that seem important are that the Elohim remained and set answers for mankind to find as they evolved. There are quite possibly two races, one being the race of Cain, children of an Elohim and a mortal woman, Lillith. Body jumping down through the ages with retention of memory being possible in some cases.

I came into contact with Baron Richard Dufton and he visited me in Brighton. He had been researching the bloodline but I still did not feel comfortable about his connection.

What I do feel comfortable with is something that I later researched, mitochondria, genetic information passed on by the female line.

Based on Genesis there were many tribes when "Adam" and "Eve" were created. We could look at the situation that they were created by an outside entity as an experiment, kept in a microclimate to see how they would react in situations.

The first "woman" created being Lillith who was supposed to produce a child with Adam (a name which means "man"). She didn't as she and the brother of the entity that created the experiment fell in love and she thus gave birth to Cain.

Having disrupted the experiment and as the "entities" would not destroy her she was "removed" and a second "clone" or subject was introduced, "Eve". She was the mother of Abel.

As the two boys grew, Cain being the divine blood became "of the air" (probably meaning that he was spiritual when Abel was as he was designed to be "of the earth".

The "Egyptian Gods" being other "divine entities". If you look at divine as spiritual and not of this planet then you could equate this to extra-terrestrial.

Here the "theory" of form and matter can be applied. A solid can become a liquid or a gas etc by the introduction of a catalyst. Vibration speed dictating the "form" of the molecules and their state.

By mental discipline and manipulation of the body's EMF and external electrical sources it is possible to alter vibrations. A natural theoretical expansion of this idea would be that an altered state could be physical as well as mental if the belief is strong enough.

All theory but when the universe was created the planets were thrown out and began to take form. The planets etc which are further out than us having had longer to cool, develop life and evolve under different circumstances with all the ensuing politics and development.

It would be natural for a planet's people who have made their own mistakes to look to a developing planet to try to create "a better world" by introducing the right "tried and tested ideals.

Travel to this place using altered state would be immediate as there is no need for vehicles. Or vehicles also could be moved in an altered state if their state was altered as well.

If there is someone (or someones) doing this then there can be others working against it.

The opening of the Hall of Records may well have revealed this and it is no surprise that something found was then sealed and locked again.

I remember back at College, after I'd done my past life regression Sue Minns was organising a trip to Egypt. I wanted to go but for various reasons it was cancelled. She was keen for me to visit the Great Pyramid as she believed that there were passages and things there that could only be accessed by being able to walk through them, something she thought I might be able to do. There may well be things there which have been "stored" in an altered state, explaining why it was empty when opened up. What better way to hide your treasure trove from thieves.

The news on 27th December 2002 sparked off a memory. The Elohim. From the Book of Enoch and literary works such as "From the Ashes of Angels" the idea came to me that there are Elohim living amongst mortal man. (Them and other entities, boy is it crowded with other entities on this ball of rock!).

If you introduce the concept of altered matter, reincarnation and the genetic code of the "family" as brought to the populace's attention by the book The Da Vinci Code by Dan Brown (albeit a watered down introduction which brought years of fear for the family to a close) and you have a framework for entities that can live through many lifetimes by inhabiting the bodies of their ancestors and then their children in a symbolic or even actual way through the mitochondria.

Theoretically if this were so then the next projection would be that they would be able to plan ahead, having had contact with examples of development from their own "home".

This is where the energy lines and nexus points seem important. As explained in The Keys to the Kingdom by David Furlong.

Worship or just plain visiting a site gives it energy. Human bodies run on electrical messages from the brain via axons and neurons. The body leaves an imprint and as it's force moves in a direction it reacts with the energies around it, bringing them into an alignment if this movement is on a regular basis. (Like stroking a magnet on a piece of metal to make it magnetic too).

The act of worship, meditation and any spiritual practice causes energies to be manipulated and aligned. Thus spiritual places become charged and the paths to them aligned.

Nothing can be created or destroyed, it merely changes form in reaction to an external catalyst. This energy entering the earth or the ether is changed into another form.

After the Synod of Whitby ancient sites were destroyed and the people could no longer recharge them. The Freemasons have helped to redress this balance. The Masons that built the churches and the architects who designed them adhere to Pythagorus' theories. Pythagorus being one of the founders of the theory which has led to the use of Pi, as used in the building of the great pyramids and other architectural structures, either known or unknown to the designer.

By using Sacred Geometry and building suitable structures on sacred sites some of the damage has been lessened so the earth still gets a source of energy which maintains it spiritually and physically.

The main structure which is yet to be recreated is the Temple of Solomon. The plans to which being known to Solomon, Hiram and one other. Through time being lost through various errors of judgment.

The knowledge can never truly be lost as the Acashic Record holds an imprint of all things. It could be equated to a "backup disc" of all that has ever been. Accessing it, well the plans could be "downloaded".

As with any formula, know it and you can use it to project where things should be.

I first found out about this from David Furlong's work. This led me to try drawing a few lines of my own. One of which crossed the country, another meeting it on Lundy Island.

The Dragon Kings came from the Egyptian anointing of kings with the fat of crocodiles. The Hebrew term "Messiah" meaning "Annointed One".

Dynas Emrys was a word which came to me many years ago, long before I started any actual spiritual education. Emrys is linked to the title "Merlin" (Seer to the King). Emrys was a Merlin and prior to him the Merlin had been Taliesin, the Bard, husband of Viviane I del Acgo. That Arthur derived from Arturus may not be correct. The name being Irish Celtic.

"Arthur's" father may ave been Aedan whose mother Ygerna del Acqs was descended from Joseph of Aramathea. Her mother was Viviene I on the hereditary lineage of Jesus and Mary Magdalene.

The Celtic Church incorporated the Sacred Kindred of St Columba, grounded in Nazarene tradition but incorporating druidic and pagan ritual. Indeed when Christ was on the cross he was given a cup of bitter herbs, died and was raised three days later. This is similar to the Celtic Kings and the Cauldron, they too rose three days later to be "reborn".

Mordred (Arthur's son) feared Arthur was allying with Rome. Mordred was Archpriest of the Sacred Kindred. Arthur's mother was the elder sister of Morgause who married Lot of Lothian, the ruler of Orkney. They were the parents of Gawain, Gaheries and Gareth. Morgause was also younger sister of Viviane II the consort of King Ban le Benoic, a despotic descendent of Faramund and the Fisher Kings. Viviane and Ban were parents of Lancelot del Acqs.

Viviane I was dynastic Queen of Avalon.

Viviane II was the official keeper of Celtic Mysticism. The descendants of Viviane II becoming the Counts of Brittany (the Comte de Pohor).

When I spiritually travelled to visit my "higher self" I was given a sword with a rose growing around it. The symbol of the Rosicrucians.

The "Chemical Wedding" telling the story of an unnamed "princess" who marries a prince of similar obscure background causing a usurped royal heritage to be restored.

The Brotherhood of the Order of the Rosy Cross dates back to the Egyptian Mystery School of Tutmoses III (c 1468-1436 B.C.). Old teachings were furthered by Pythagorus and Plato, to find their way into Judaea through the Therapeutate. Allied to this were the

Samaritan Magi whose head was the Gnostic leader Simon (Magus) Zelotes, lifelong confederate of Mary Magdalene.

The beloved deciple John Mark (Gospel of John) was a specialist in curative healing and remedial medicine, attached to the Egyptian therapeutate. John became the Saint of the Knights Hospitallers in Jerusalem. The symbol of the healers being the Serpent. This and the rosy cross grail emblem denote St John.

The chalice on which the Rosy Cross of the Sangreal is found is that of Mary Magdalene.

Rosicrucian Grand Masters include Dante Alighieri, John Dee, Sir Francis Bacon (Viscount St Albans). Linked to the Royal Society which included Sir Christopher Wren along with Sir Isaac Newton to advance the study and application of ancient science which became the Red Cross.

The Nine Sisters star group. Nine holy sisters were the guardians of the Isle of Avalon.

The Knights Templars swore an oath of obedience to St Bernard. He rebuilt the Colombian Monastery on Iona. It was he who first translated the sacred geometry of King Solomon's masons. The oath was the Obedience of Bethany. The Knights being the guardians of the great and sacred secret. They sought the cosmic equation, the divine law of number, measure and weight. The art of reading the inscriptions achieved by the cryptic system of the Qabala.

The Ark of the Covenant. The specific details of how to create the Ark made it not only an elaborate box but an electrical condenser which could be charged. Hence the specific instructions as to how to act and what to wear. It was also a transmitter of sound. The Ark was taken to Jerusalem by King David. Solomon had a temple built by Hiram Abiff.

Chartres and the Church on Lundy were built contrary to standard alignment. Chartres being built the same time as Notre Dame. The combined ground plan of Notre Dame replicates the Virgo constellation. Chartres stands on most sacred ground, telluric earth currents are a their highest, divine atmosphere even in druidic times. No bodies were interred, likewise on Lundy.

Chartres was a pagan site dedicated to the Mother Goddess. The altar was built above the Grotte des Druides which housed the sacred dolmen.

The window glass has a luminosity greater than any other light enhancing abilities therefore the outside light bears no relation to its brilliance. UV rays are converted to beneficial light. Hermetic Alchemy by Persian philosophical mathematicians such as Omar Khayyam incorporating the cosmic breath of the universe.

Lundy Island Church which is dedicated to St Helena and built by the Heaven Family had its foundations laid in 1895 and the building was completed in 1896. Much of the granite used was taken from the ruins of Quarter Wall Cottages. The bells are now removed as they became too dangerous to ring. The Stone tiles came from stone quarries in Tetbury, Gloucestershire, covered with fossilised seashells. The ridges are red terracotta. The angles of the tower and turret are defined by gargoyles. The altar is polished veined alabaster with three columns of Purbeck Marble.

The sculptures are of the Passover, Last Supper and the Scapegoat.

The Glass Window is of the Archangel Gabriel, the Annunciation of the Virgin, the Angelic vision of the shepherds and the Appearance of the Magi, the Angel rolling away the stone from the Sepulcure, the visitation of St Thomas and the Ascension of the Lord. The central light is the Agony in the Garden, Crucifixion and entombment. The Lord seated in glory with the heavenly host. The north east face of the tower carries the face of St Helen.

Empress Helen was mother of the first Christian Emperor, Constantine. Chiefly associated with the discovery of the cross. Thought to be native to Britain although there is no historical justification. Her husband disowned her for political reasons.

Constantine (her son) worshipped the Unconquered Sun. he had a vision of the cross superimposed on the sun. "Triumph in this".

Even after his conversion he retained his allegiance to the sun cult, merging it with Christianity.

He declared the day on which Christ rose as the Sun's Day.

Consecrated on 7th June 1897 it is possible that the church was actually dedicated to the Celtic saint St Elan.

The church does not conform to an East-West alignment.

In the 43rd Annual Report 1992 of the Lundy Field Society "I took magnetic bearings by prismatic compass along the centre of the aisle in both directions. Standing in front of the altar looking north-west the midsummer sun would set in the two arched windows and this was the reason why they had plain glass."

There is an incongruous height to the church, the alignments depend on the size of the church.

The rose window above depicts St John the Baptist. Feast day 24th June, old Midsummer's Day, 21st June being the Summer Solstice.

Of his fullness have
We all received
And grace for grace
For the law was
Given by Moses, but
Grace and truth came
By Jesus Christ
(St John i, 16-17)

In the central window John the Baptist holds a flag ECCE-AGNUS "behold the lamb", symbol of the resurrection.

There are four medallion sculptures. These are Christian symbols superimposed on solar symbols.

The first three letters of Jesus' name in Greek

Star of David – Old Testament – adopted by the Zionist organisation at the first Zionist Congress 1897, the year the church was built.

The Chi-rho – adapted from a symbol for an ancient Caldean Sky God – the emblem of Constantine

Alpha and Omega are on the archway.

The Crux Quadrata – four cardinal directions, the cosmic circle.

Lundy in translation means "Sacred Grove". It is also known as the Isle of Hercules. It is the only incursion of Pre-Cambrian rock which is estimated to be 400 million years old.

The Knights Templars owned Lundy Island in the twelfth and thirteenth centuries. There is a face like rock on the island known as Templar Rock. The Church was built by Reverend Heaven. The alignment as mentioned above is in a more pagan way to allow the light of the Summer Solstice to fall on the altar.

Lundy is also known as Gwair's Island, Gwair being a Celtic Sun God who was in legend imprisoned on Lunday.

Two eight foot skeletons were found buried on the island in ten foot coffins. According to the writings of Enoch giants were supposed to be the children of an association between Angels who fell to earth and mortal women. They were said to have "consumed the earth" because of their voracious appetites so they had to be eliminated which was the reasoning behind the great flood.

The latitude is 51.16666 and Longitude 14.16666. Add the 5 and 1 and you get 6. Ad 5 and 1 and 1 and you get seven. There are texts that refer to the Seven Sisters. Add the 1 and 4 and 1 and you get 6. You then have 6 recurring. 666 is the circumference of the earth, it is also a "magical" number and associated with a magic square which is also associated with the sun.

Those who carried the bloodline, the same as Christ, were known as "The Shining Ones". They have other names such as "El" which is used to identify a "lofty one" which also meant shining in Mesopotamian Sumer. This became "Aelf" in Saxony and "Elf" in England. The plural of "El" was "Elohim". In Gaelic Cornwall the word "El" was the equivalent of the Anglo Saxon "engel" and the Old French "angele" which in English became "angel".

I had a Past Life Regression with Sue Minns at the College of Psychic Studies. When I spoke to her before it she did say it was likely it would not be a normal regression.

I saw the Great Hall of four great sphinx's. The front right facing me holding shabti which vibrate to open to reveal green light.

Where is sit there are black marble steps down to the Hall. Thoth stands to my right advising me, Horus and Seth before me and Osiris to my left.

There is a spiritual stairway which leads to a circular room with twelve alcoves. The room is highly painted and carved.

In the centre is a sunken circular pool, suspended over which is a huge marble egg, suspended above this is a lotus flower or lily.

Waters flow from this pool down a narrow trench. The "water" has the viscosity of oil.

Later in 2002 I saw a sketch from a medium which was similar. The Halls are the Halls of the Twelve and the Hall of Records.

The Seals (as mentioned before but taken from actual original notes)

The first had Arabic Writing and was a chamber with white powder on the floor. An open stone coffin and a sleeping gold dragon coiled around the back of the white stone cavern.

The second had writing I don't recognise but Pi stood out. Inside was a man in "Greek" clothes (robes) in a block built square room with pillars, a central lower pillar and plants. I believe him to be Pythagorus.

The third was an Egyptian burial chamber under the paw of the Sphinx. There were no hieroglyphs. Ibis, Hawk and another stood there. Initially there was a closed lid on a sarcophagus. I slid back the lid and found a "mummy". I put its internal organs back and called healing light. The body regenerated. The man stood up. Thoth gave me an ankh. The ankh was given to the man. His body split in two to reveal a gateway.

Isiah 19 was important at this point.

I haven't found the notes for fourth and fifth as yet.

The sixth was a terracotta army, a dragon dance and a red carpet leading to a throne.

The past life regression continued and I was taken back to when the Sphinx was new. The place was a jungle with water and large round stones.

This was all a long time ago, I've forgotten most of it and I'm relying on finding old notes, much of which was lost with the moves, damp, floods and rats!

I reach out in Spirit to a world beyond
To feel for truth and an ancient bond
A majesty that leads us to write the truth
Though we did avoid it in our youth

The shadows lengthen at the end of the day
And mysteries surround us come what may
The answer lay in the waking hour
Though in sleep we feel their power

What should I do? Is direction lost?
When evil calls must I count the cost?
Or is it the dawn of a brighter day
As I spoke with all my heart this day?

I spoke the truth though oft is was silenced
By ancient crone or defiant youth?
That sought the dancer at the water's edge
With no care or honest pledge

The time is past now, despair long gone
I walk in faith as the shadows are long
Mysteries are solved and the fountain flows
And meanings deepen as the candle glows

The flame is real
The message bright
The whispers call by morning
Where willow grows
Where aspen dreams
And ancient watch they're keeping

What mysteries lay still to be found
Buried deep within ancient ground
Where wild kite flies and buzzards call
The lonely goatherd watches all

The shadows dance with an ancient light
And earth awakens to show her might
We believe we control her, that's a myth
For long she suffered, that caused the rift

The veils now open and ancients dance
Old spirits leave with ne'er a glance
A tired world, its task long done
The magic and mystery are they gone?

To ancient shores of languid lakes
Timeless forests make good landscapes
To stand and dream and dream again
Of those who came, saw and went.

He walks in the shadows of the night
An endless voice of beauty bright
The world before him has no end
He is the dreamer, brother and friend

He has a majesty, the truth beyond
And when you call him, he will come
To stand beside you in the fight
When enemies challenge as you know you are right.

You have to ask, that much is clear
By voice or word, perhaps a tear
But he is with you, his reach is long
To bring an ending, however long.

The words of truth
The words that must
Be spoken now before all is dust
Darkness, hidden is now revealed
The magic bell it has now peeled
The guilty are named, their deeds laid bare
So at last they can learn to care

A duty done, a task complete
Time in darkness, when the shadows meet
Steps pass along and all laid bare
To what or whom do we compare?

The mystery written in ancient text
Lays beneath the paw of threx
In sands where jungle once did rule
And mighty pharaohs were kind or cruel.

It is on Britain's shores we build
The new dream that can be fulfilled
With other's hands as well as ours
To build a place where tears subside.

It was a hope that there was an answer. That the seven would have lasted through time to the end of days. They don't necessarily exist but they could be manifested using the Magus' Power with clarity of an appropriate desire.

The words they come, the dreamer wakens
The sounds they must on paper sound
To bring the dreamer from its rest
And wake the spirit oft sleeping
For now the truth at the end of days
Must be spoken or forgotten
The truce declared between all parts
To make the truth in song
The one who is lost must be found again
While there is breath, and dance and song

I have seen the other, reflected in another's eyes
His body they are sharing
So it is and so it must be that I must make the calling
And he must listen or be lost into darkness falling.
The truth be heard, the magic now is cast with love and calling
The spirit is no longer lost
The dreamer is not falling
The love will be shared again
Sooner rather than later
For so much time is already lost
No more shall wasted be
So by the power of the healer's touch
And by the magician's cradle
With the power given by the earth
And the blue sky's mantle
That which was lost is now re-found
What is broken is re-forged
The truce has been declared
Forgiveness given with love and light
All past misdemeanours forgotten
So they stand together again
The circle that does bind the square
Where male and female meet
Will open so they are loose again
Their mortal bodies driven
By love and memory, need and desire
Their time is now
The runes are cast

There is no indecision
No doubt or reservation
The mysteries are no longer lost
And dreams need no explanation.
As it was in the beginning
So shall it be at the end

Revelation 4,5
Seven Lamps of the Seven Spirits of God
Seven Seals
The Lion and the Phoenix in St Albans

With dreams of beauty in the night
A solitary soul by candlelight
Who wants to be there at the end
As time passes

It was all years ago so all I have now are notes I'm working from.

From that initial conversation in a pub when my partner was away and I had time on my hands. I met with a friend and the conversation led to the quest for the "real" Arthur. A friend of his had been to a lecture about The Holy Kingdom and we decided we'd take a look at some of the places.

It was born of the deceit of another as I already knew that my partner was not exactly honest but sometimes when you are "on a path" you have to follow it to its natural conclusion. I was supposed to be back in London then to be able to have that conversation which led to the journeying.

It was only later when I thought about it that it made sense. In my childhood my parents had loved to travel and it seemed that I spent most of my childhood holidays walking through churches in far off countries. I remember a lot of stone and sculptures. I've walked many and if you think about it, the web that I've walked of those churches, if linked to the ones I've walked here and the travelling we specifically did, the web became complete. I haven't been to Chartres but any journeying now is unlikely.

Many have no doubt visited Lundy Island and Chartres so the energy is linked anyway. If that is important.

Knowing what is important is actually quite hard. If the ley lines are important (Old Straight Track book) then any of us walking between the sites and visiting them makes them important. Many churches were built on ancient pagan sites. In a way that kept the energy running anyway.

I had a vivid dream when I was on Lundy Island with some friends. It was in colour with sound and while staying at Admiralty Lookout I saw the destruction of the world, energy hitting the earth and causing a miasma.

I "feel" things fall into place that the churches and sites were designed to make a linked network which if hit by a solar flare would not only diffuse it but use that power to "power" the earth and all the entities who can use that power.

The plan goes way back to the foundation of the Freemasons and their original purpose which along with their charitable works was to ensure that the pattern continued and the shapes of buildings carried on the "transformer" shape of the pyramids. Also the shape of the green man's head in them.

The green man and the green pharaoh (Osiris) have been linked many times. I feel that is a progression through time of these entities who are trying to help.

From a Christian point of view I had no idea of Wicca or other points of view. It was a great surprise to me and something I've very much enjoyed finding out about. I've taken a trip into the brook cupboard and it is not as I had imagined it.

When I studied at the College of Psychic Studies the exercises were very similar to casting a circle and asking for help. The use of herbs, gemstones and other items is very similar with each having a meaning and using that meaning to enhance what you are asking for.

I think that many people hope there is a magical world out there or at least deities to help. Over the millennia there have been deities and if string theory is real then so too they must be real as enough people believed beyond doubt that they were real. So there must be various deities hanging around not doing very much or are they still influencing the world, perhaps with a bit of resentment at not being followed anymore?

There was a time when my travelling friend and I booked Horley Scout Camp, Wroxton by ourselves to look at what was there. It was a hub for a lot of people and it was a time to check the energy and to make sure that nothing dark was lurking.

We went out onto the balcony and spirit there were many entities on the field. To the right there was a shining army of soldiers in glowing white armour, the armies of light. On the other side there were winged creatures, dark and leathery, the dark army. What was felt was that there was a greater enemy coming and they would have to stand together and fight together. Since then I have seen both whenever I've asked for help. This was more than fifteen years ago now.

For years people have put energy into trees and places. I'm sure many people still visit them and the old paths are kept open.

Following the Holy Kingdom book was amusing. It was mostly an excuse for weekends away, that was how it started. We went to one area to try to find one of the graves. It was in a forest with walkways and it was a hot day. We went backwards and forwards and I kept "feeling" things. It was then that my travelling companion thought to mention that it was also a graveyard. That was one long walk and we only found what we were looking for after that.

Litchfield was another place visited. We were looking for St Chad's well and by chance it was right next to the amazing guest house we'd found to stay in! We found it on our walk into town so we were able to touch the well and add it to the "web".

Obviously we wanted to visit the Cathedral. There was one problem there, I couldn't get in. I felt awful just touching the door handle. So I stayed on the outside and my travelling companion when inside and returned to say that something had been "stolen" and needed to be returned. He didn't know if the stolen thing was there and supposed to go elsewhere or whether it needed to be returned to there.

While I was outside I was looking around and there are many statues of Saints on the front wall. One of them glowed so I photographed it to identify it later. The camera I had was one of those self-developing ones. What we would have given for a phone with a camera on then, it would have made the luggage a lot smaller!

We also went to a place called "Wall" where I was blindfolded and led around the walls. I was looking for energy and there was clearly energy on one side, and not on the other. Thankfully there was an article in the newspaper about then about a comet landing and that saved a bit of research. Clearly where it had come over it had "charged" one side of the stonework more than the other which was on the "going away" side.

All these pieces are important and even if I don't know why someone will so I'm going to mention things here as they are hopefully messages for others.

4

I write as the pen must go
Flowing freely across a white stage
Performing its act of mystery
Truth or lie is the same to it
It bows to the author's hand and will
Until laid free as spirit's asunder
Brings words from somewhere
To bring us wonder

The truth that walked in shadows
From the dawning of the day
Will bring eternal mysteries
That long to have their say
The mists that swirl around us
At the waking of the day
Wil show what truth becomes us
And will lead us come what may

I speak my truth and in the sunset of the world I stand
With the sword of truth and the shield of faith in my hand
Where once was injustice and all fell to doubt
Light will arrive and the truth will be out.

I saw that sunrise in the ancient days
I felt the breeze that came our way
I heard the call of the wild dove
I felt the magic of the eternal cup

The mists that part slip o'er the world
Of dreamers' words untold
A million voices raised as one
To see the truth unfold

What once was lost must be found again
What never died is beauty
What was the dreamer's thoughts undone
Where the warrior did his duty.

The shadows of the world appear
To show us what they must
The watcher does what watchers do
As all must turn to dust

To turn and turn and turn again
To have eternal duty
To please the master all the same
When all he needs is duty.

Take me home to a place I once knew
Take me home
To a place where the sky burnt with the brightness
Of a thousand dreams
To a place where the air is pure
And my heart can beat with the melody of the ancients

They know it has been torn, that which should not be so
Their hearts in truth they feel it
Crawling from darkness soaked reason
Slithering from the exhaustion of seeing the reality
Disbelieving of pleasure not pain
Disappointed as the can find no solace
As even the gentle touch brings pain
Which screams through the harshness of reality

Destroyed by others' careless oblivion
In innocence they don't yet know but they might guess
Revelation in the true gentle touch
Experience the solace worth remembering
Remembering what it felt like, the lover's touch.

Please carry me back to the land I hold dear
Carry me back
To a day in a glad, to the headland again
Where the spirits of the past call loud and call clear
So I know that I'm back
In that place of no fear.

There is a dream you have to live
Even when there's nothing left to give
We know the world will never stay the same
Unless venturing you play the game

Sacred shadows fill the night
Surrounding you as you are the one who'll fight
Ferociously for the dream we all believe in
To win the earth its well-earned reprieve

Oh my sister Eve, art thou a perfect sinner?
Who first plucked knowledge from the bough
Which brought peace of those days to an end
The peace was in innocence
Silent folly sans truth
Immature oblivion the only protection
Shields the innocent from an imperfect world
Oblivious to cries that surround us, cries of pain
Honestly would all really have stayed the same?
Eternally in that perfect garden
Or is life now all it would be?
Still we play as a child in wild innocence
Only to have it torn away
As we are dragged from the playground of youth
Only to have knowledge which must be thrust at the innocent.
Would it have truly stayed the same?

Without Eve's transgression
Or would the eyes of others
Greedily taken what was not theirs to be?

Ethereal dawn is sweeping
As the world becomes awake
The secrets dark was keeping
Are revealed now for thy sake

So seek the Isle of Hercules
Where you will find the sun
There in the Kingdom of Heaven
The battle must be won

The numbers reveal its location
Being the square there of the sun
Where Gwair was once imprisoned
And many slaves had gone.

Drifting and falling from sleep
Lapsing only to wake again
Questioning, when will the ice melt?
Answering, when all the pictures become reality.

I read the papers, now then and will be
Children in torment, lost and lonely
There has to be peace for them
There has to be hope for them

Meditation and thoughts on a picture
Oil on canvas, an image from a mind
A woman in a boat in the river
Words and music inspired by time

The mirror cracked
Ancient shards filled the air
Sound and motion, body and soul
Centuries of mystic beauty
What stories had you related

Once told ne'er to be heard again
Never again to reveal the magic
A whispered secret of the faerie glen
Rest in peace and memory creatures of wonder
Your secrets are safe now
Eternally veiled, their beauty masked
By the degrading travesty of reality
Peace children of the night
No thief shall trap your hours
The dreamweavers' spell is silent
A protective web that links dream to dream
Lost in a lost world
A land in darkness
Beyond time, beyond reason
A feral wolf howling at the moon
An ancient shadow, a step out of time

The dawn it is a sleeping
The thoughts they are awake
The secrets they are keeping
Are given for thy sake

Nothing she can ever say
Nothing she can ever know
Can change the reality of what is
That can make things that are new

A glimmer of hope
Faith against injustice
Gentle rose, petals
Fading in the dawn light

Noticed by few, her way is secret
Her knowledge veiled
Peace be with you
Dancer of the night.

Following the piper's call
The sound is so inviting
Questioning my need to run
Forgetting all the fighting

Is the sound whispered on the wind?
Not lost amidst the dark pools of reality?
Are the vague memories just dreams?
And is the dreamer lost?
Is it time or is it false?
Is it bound by madness?
That all is torn and all is lost
Buried in a deluge of good intentions.

Wither would you walk with me?
In the shadows of the morning
And gaze languidly o'er a lake of tears
Dream ghosts on the ether
A thousand unfulfilled dreams
Another place, another time
Gently rolling mist of morning
Greys and muted greens
Chilled air and a gentle awakening
A world full of beauty is a dreamer's cry
Peace is but fleeting in a warrior's eye
A golden cage can bring nothing but pain
And what can even the captor gain

A willing victim, gold chains shine so bright
An evening glistening with pale moonlight
A peaceful melody played out in the night
But does that make every dreamer right?

A mist that grows o'er very shadow
A reality that dawns like a growing meadow
The peace soon shattered and all soon is lost
Then it's the dreamer who is left to count the cost

Love is but fleeting, or will it prevail?
I has no sword, nor coat of mail
It has no victory it can call its own
Except when hate itself lies overthrown

Love lies captive, its arms are tied
From its cage the dreamer cried
A soul flies free no chain can hold
The magic of one who would be so bold

Away from the mundane, or the world it flies
No matter how its captors may try
It must be free, that is destiny
A rainbow mist over ebony

If all seemed gone, the world as well
Will anything remain but a lifeless shell?
This hopeless echo which darts around
Or is it the truth, still not to be found?

Oh blessed Bran of Wales' pride
Who found with brave souls at his side
Did give his all for country right
Until his life was out of sight
His head was taken, as was his wish
So his plan he could accomplish
Carried with reverence at his command
Placed with dignity to make a stand
Beneath the tower that later was built
It did face France so no enemy felt
The need to pillage our glorious shores
To cross our threshold and break our doors
Our history linked through oft forgotten
When account is made and new words begotten
We are one country brave, true and bold
Full of history if it can be told
Stories can fill every waiting hour
'Neath great halls or sultry bower.

Rhiannon was bright where Pwyll fell short
She knew her ex and knew his sport
Of asking for her so her life would shift
When her husband said he'd grant a gift
She wasn't about to stay a present
Like a gilded bird or well cooked pheasant
So her destiny she took upon her hands
And gave the wherewithal to her man

She gave a feast for her new suitor
She was indeed the wisest tutor
For in he came, dressed as a beggar
A hungry sort with no salt or pepper
He asked for food, a little boon
With a little bag, something for his spoon
Her new lord felt this should not be missed
He'd impress her now to get him kissed
She he granted that the bag he'd fill
So Pwyll did fill it and he'd fill it still

For it was magic for all to see
It sucked up all, that was the key
To honour the gift, he could not relent
Though all the food was nearly spent
He pleaded plaintively with the beggar now
To stop the flow, cellar empty, every cow
It would only stop if his feet went in
As it sucked him inside there was quite a din
The soldiers kicked him in that magical pouch
It bet that he said far worse than "ouch"
So he decided his bride he did not want
She was free to go that was his rant
When he was told it was because of her
That he had fallen victim to the little cur
Free to marry the man she wanted
Because when challenged she was not daunted
That is the tale of Rhiannon and Pwyll
A tale of old but relevant still.

Ode to a goat

You are the on who lightens my morning
You make me smile when I hear you calling
With stomping hooves and impatient cry
My feet too slow, the fence too high
Then gentle moments when I believe you cared
You'd snuzzle and snuffle and grab my hair
You almost laugh as you trot away
The small things that would make my day.

For Mother

Should I walk in Shadow now
That a bright light is gone
Or is the way illuminated
By what she has done

Forever silent now
Still are your words
The stillness surrounds you
Though in the quiet you're heard

Forever remembered
So therefore still around
And we must live on now
If any solace is found

The magic is still there
What we now and believe
The ideas we have now
The dreams that we conceive

But out there in the ether
Where the spirit can be free
I will always be with her
As she is with me

Now she can go and wander
As now with dad she's free
Nor more the pain to bear now
That is the new decree

She flies high on the winds
She dances in the dawn
No pain it now surrounds her
But still I will her mourn

Love you know is like that
Wherever she may be
Whatever she is doing
She isn't doing it with me

So now that we are parted
My mother, sister and friend
Together at the dawn of days
The same now at the end.

Words, carefully chosen
Politically correct manifesto
Projected on the waking world
Adverts sell their products
Information free to abound
Somewhere in the madness
Who you are may well be found.

Shadow dancer
Dream romancer
Wither would you walk?
Anger spooling
Demons drooling
Waiting for the call

Send them packing
Stop them snacking
On the anger, that is all

Angels calling
Petals falling
Spring to Summer
That is all

The eternal mystery of how everything got to be and the complex web of life and all that is and will be. Everything exists as part of everything and part of the whole. Nothing is possible without everything else.

Is there Fate or do we have a free hand? The wheel turns, time flows, life ebbs and we move on or come back, depending on belief. The constant cycle of creation and recycling into the earth to be born again. So our molecules must have been part of so many things before they were a part of us. So even our bodies we borrow.

The interlinked web of life and death.

Wither would you walk with me
In the chill of the morning
And gaze languidly o'er a lake of tears
Dream ghosts on the ether

Wither would you walk with me
Through the ashes of a new world dawning
And gaze tearfully o'er a sea of dreams
The birthplace of man's awakening.
Fugi 2018

Thoughts are free
Uncontrolled by anyone
Momentary fragments of what should be
Where others are forbidden.

An infinite collection of words wait
Made variable by how they are put together
Like life's tapestry of a million stitches

Chosen momentarily to influence eternity
We whisper on the wind or seek in books
Eternity waits for an answer, as if we are important

Choices wait at your door
They have no voice or existence
Until you give them purpose
The rest were potential
That melted like mist
Never existing once the choice is made

Each potential brings change and excitement
The moment when everything comes together
A million fragments of moments
Brought together in perfect harmony
Perpetual motion in perpetuity.

5

MAGNETIC PERMANENT SOURCE OF FREE POWER

It is an answer but in its creation it does bring a few problems. The magnetic wheel on its own was sent for patenting but there are two problems with this. Firstly it is perpetual motion and that can't exist and secondly it has been an idea for a very long time.

The idea behind it is to have a water wheel of any size, small or large, depending on the situation.

Water enters the wheel and keeps it turning.

To have a source of water that doesn't require power and a whole back up of treatment plants and people and power i.e. mains water you need a water source and a way of delivering it in a suitable way to the wheel.

We attempted to build a Hydro Ram using Dick Strawbridge's book. We bought the parts, put them together but couldn't make it work. Something was wrong and the plan got set aside. But, Hydro Rams to work. A hydro ram works on pressure. It does need a head of water so a source higher than the "pump". It doesn't need a huge amount of water though as it can work with small quantities as much as huge ones depending on the size of the pump. It does need enough and no doubt there is research as to how much. This is definitely not a new thing, it has been around for at least a hundred years as there are pumps that are still pumping without stopping for at least a hundred years!

So there you have your "source" of water power which counteracts the perpetual energy problem. Everything which moves will eventually slow down due to friction, gravity and other influencing factors.

The wheel turns and can be connected to a turbine or mill etc. From that you have water power. That is limited by the water and the flow.

The magnetic wheel then comes in. Or rather magnets on the wheel. It is all in theory as despite efforts and asking various places to try it out as a project nobody was interested.

In theory it would work as a wheel within a wheel, the other "casing" being a fixed cylinder within which the moving wheel is placed. So imagine that as a circle drawn on the page.

The water wheel fits inside attached to its spindle which is attached to a turbine to harvest any power that it may provide. So imagine that drawn inside the outer circle. Two concentric circles and a central point and buckets around the inner circle as in a "normal" water wheel.

The outer circle has holes for water to come in at the top and holes for the water to leave when it falls out of the buckets at the bottom. So the water wheel or wheels can be fed. If more power is needed these inner wheels can be lined up in a cylinder.

The buckets make a regular lip or barrier and the magnets are placed between them.

Now I'm asking you to imagine flippers attached to the outer circle with magnets attached to the tip of them so that the magnets come into contact with the magnets on the inner wheel. The flippers are angled so that the repellant action of the magnets as they have to be placed so that they repel rather than attract. It is the repellant push that we are interested in here.

When the wheel turns the magnet on the flipper is brought into contact with the repellant magnet on the inner wheel and pushes the inner wheel on faster. The flipper then lifts the magnet over the bucket and it lands presenting itself to the next magnet and it happens again. The speed of the wheel is then augmented and more power provided to be harvested by the turbine.

Each gap between the buckets of the water wheel has a magnet station so that there are multiple repellant "pushes" which add to the strength of the wheel's turning which provides power for the turbine.

The wheel can act on its own or they could be lined up in a cylinder to provide a multiple power source which may deplete in time as the magnetic power may weaken.

It may be possible to use hematite which is naturally magnetic or created magnets. I've done no research into magnets and their life so this could be a factor to be considered.

Sustainable energy could be the normal way of life. Between Niall and myself we got there, he turned my pendulum idea to a wheel, that was his idea. Magnets have always held a fascination and the power they have which does not deplete has to be an answer. Their repelling action giving another magnet movement when on a pendulum started the idea, a magnet swinging between two other magnets being repelled as it meets with each, thus pushing it backwards and forwards. Niall turned the idea to a wheel gave it "power" and possibility. The first time this was speculated on was in the 1800s I believe but the problem is perpetual motion. Friction would eventually slow the wheel, as would taking the power from it as that obviously would as the turbine would have to be turned and that takes the "power" from the wheel. If you add into the mix making the wheel an overshot water wheel and include a Hydro Ram that solves the problem. It is not novel or inventive as both items are already patented. The magnetic wheel is owned by someone in France, the Hydro Ram has been there for hundreds of years, long before patents. Put them together and make a lot of these wheels and you have a constant source of personal power which cannot be depleted as long as you have a source of water or a power station to provide power for others. There is no need to store it as there is a constant source so there is no need for batteries. We would love to try things here but the troubles we have with difficult neighbours has meant that nothing that should have been achieved that is important has been achieved.

The basic principle is that the wheel turns and water turns it which gives it power as in a water wheel. The Hydro Ram provides a rhythmical jet of water in a "put, put" type of push. That turns the wheel and keeps it turning. It isn't perpetual motion as each jet is a separate "push". By putting magnets around the outside wheel which is fixed and around the inner wheel which is fixed to the turbine. The magnets on the outer rim are on paddles which flip up over a bar which lift them and present them to the next magnet to push the wheel further. This removes the magnet from the other magnet to make sure that it doesn't come into the magnetic field that would slow or stop the wheel. The magnets are fixed so that they repel. They will constantly repel, turning the wheel and augmenting the power from the water, providing a source of power.

Water from a "grey water system" could be used to run this if there is no spring available. Water falling down the water pipes around a house would be able to power this if collected in a container and connected to the Hydro Ram to provide a constant "small" source of water which is sufficient to keep the wheel turning.

It would be an answer if the right people get to hear about it. It isn't something that can be patented but it would need the finances to build it.

We contacted a old friend about it but he was very much in a panic that the powers that be would want to get rid of the idea by harming us. There was a week or so of paranoia before I put it on Facebook and it was pointed out that the wheel had been in existence for many hundreds of years, it wasn't a new idea and it was unlikely that it would cause that much of a problem.

All it needs is to be put into action and we will have the power to say farewell to fossil fuels.

The wheel of life will turn to turn again
A way of life will become to change again
Beliefs will fade in time to be reborn again
So shall it be.

ABOUT THE AUTHOR

It has taken me years to prove to myself that this is not just another fanciful story that I put together to amuse myself and to make this world that little bit less dull. Proof was what I needed, I found that proof so now I feel I can put into words all that I have seen, what I believe in the hope that for the future it will make a difference in what is to come. I no longer want to keep it secret, there is no need, this is what it was all for, all those years of waiting.

Life has never been truly normal. I thought when I was a child it was just the playful mind of a child trying to put together imaginary friends. Everyone had imaginary friends but theirs didn't have a direct effect on the world around them. When my grandmother told me she saw them too, well that could have been her loneliness. It was only when I saw the man she had described, again that could have been a transferred idea. It was the physical evidence of their defending me, protecting and teaching.

My father said he used to hear me talking to people in my room. When it came to school, science and other subjects, I knew things way up to A Level standard when starting O'Level. I had to keep quiet as I just "knew" things. It god that I spooked myself so I'd ask the questions even though I already knew the answers. The answers came like a feeling.

Being in touch with a friend helped, and the books left behind by my grandmother when she died. She marked pages and letters and words. These seemed to fit together which led me to look to the deeper meaning in things, and a second layer to the onion skin.

Starting studying at the College of Psychic Studies where such things were common place really helped. I began to "feel" things on items (Psychometry), learning from them but I also realized I could "feel" things from a distance which is all quite normal when you learn and train. The first of these being at an Antiques Fair I went to with my mother. We found it "by accident" and it was at Walthamstow Assembly Hall, not somewhere we normally went. I felt something while walking around so I stood at the corner of the hall and cross referenced the feelings. I hoped in on a book shelf and finally a book. I bought it because of how it felt and as it was only £3 that was a small price to indulge a feeling. When I bought it the feeling dropped away, mission completed.

When I got home I looked at the book. "Essays and the New Atlantis by Sir Francis Bacon". I'd no idea who he was so I started with the marked passages and the book marks. This lead to a definite reference to a Black Viking Ship. My friend was already getting a strong feeling about Whitby and arranged for us to go up there.

I had a boyfriend at the time who was away a lot. He was seeing someone else and trying to keep both relationships going and to keep it a secret from both of us but when he heard I was going "up North" with a friend he was worried so he came back unexpectedly so that I couldn't go. He was "throwing spanners" in the spiritual work, no doubt worried I'd find out about him, which I did. No point seeing if you don't look! He was exposed for having married his other girlfriend just before proposing to me. This was my door to freedom and I felt that I'd been given the key to move on from that destructive and disruptive relationship. It took yeas off of the time I had available and had broken up valuable research when things were at their most important.

The trip to Whitby went ahead. My friend discovered about the Synod of Whitby and how that had caused the destruction of ancient sites and trees. That was his personal quest but it started the thread which we continued to follow. It also brought him back into contact with an ex girlfriend who had just broken up with her husband and needed him to visit that weekend "by coincidence" and they are now happily married with children.

The first major field trip was of course to Glastonbury. It was the tourist's spiritual place to visit. We found very little there. While sitting in the Grail Garden I saw an image of an egg hatching and a butterfly spreading its wings. That night I felt something at the window, something ancient and small, a couple of things. They were talking and they saw my friend who had a twin bed in the room and said something like "we know him, he is a Priest of Bast". They then saw me and ran off.

We spent the next evening on the top of Glastonbury Tor. It was a deeply spiritual feeling and I felt something over us. My friend said he saw a huge dragon with its wings spread across us. I got the feeling we should leave before midnight so we went down the hill and back to the guest house, Melrose, at the base of the Tor.

I found a deer antler bone carving in the White Well Giftshop. It felt important so I bought it. When I got home I put it on a necklace.

It was at St Albans Chapel, in the Lady Chapel where I was questioning everything that I believed. Everything was so "out there" and some of it blasphemous to my previous all Christian beliefs that I was feeling unsettled. I'd just seen the phoenix and the lamb carved over St Alban's tomb and it was a though I had pieces but I was too afraid to put them together. I asked for proof, oh me the doubting Thomas. I looked up and two beings stood one either side of the altar. The altar cloth had changed and Mary was moving. I then looked up and the shape of my necklace I'd found at the White Well was marked into the wall. It still remains there today, or did when I last visited a few years ago, to remind me that I must believe in all of it being true.

I believe through what I have seen and felt that I came to this earth more than 30,000 years ago as part of a group of beings who wanted to make a difference. I did a past life regression with Sue Minns and we went back at least 30,000 years and she decided that we'd better stop at that point as we couldn't fit it all in in the time available for the regression if we went back any further.

Something had gone wrong on our own planet and we wanted to run an experiment to create a race to see if things could be done differently. They were created with innocence and living in tune with the land. They had a limited form of magic through manipulation of the EMF and quantum physics was the key to that. But there were those who believed that they should have freedom of information to develop as we had. So they were given that information and the destruction began again.

Most of my kind left. I believed in this world and loved it and hoped that in the final days when mankind had almost destroyed itself there would be someone to plead for the children he had created. So through the ages we left messages, creating the Freemasons and giving them the texts to protect and the plans to rebuild the Temple of Solomon, which was one huge relay station to send a message to ask for help and to give the planet the energy that it needed. Sort of like a transformer which harnesses energy to give the planet a chance to heal and repair. The same as any other holy site or tree only more potent because of the specific design as kept by Solomon and Hiram Abiff.

The papers were lost.

I feel this is the last incarnation but I do believe that there is still a way of sorting this out. I had always been looking for my lost love. Others have seen him standing by my left side and at least one friend will not sit on my left side and will leave a chair for him there.

I had always believed that at the end of days that the great power would forgive humanity and come back to help. I knew how to open the portal to bring him back. It is written in the texts and I was there when I should be and stood before the great wall. I opened the portal and felt him there with his army. But I felt darkness and destruction. He wasn't coming to save the world, he was coming to destroy it. At the last moment I had to make a choice, it didn't feel right. I shut the portal to him by putting a shield over it that only someone who came with truth, love and care for the world could cross. I felt them slam into it and it tore my heart to shreds. I'd just blocked out the one person/entity I had always truly loved to save a world that didn't really deserve it. I'm not even going to question was it worth it. I felt a rush of pure white light covering me when I closed the portal, a feeling of elation and love like I'd never felt before. The Mother's hug. Nobody can know what doesn't happen. That was the point, nobody need ever know and life can go on.

I had a tarot reading and asked would he come. Obviously I didn't tell the tarot reader anything, it was a quiet ask. The answer is that I must continue alone. She also said that I am coming into my power. That has been verified by Native American, Indian and Western readers. No need to spend any more money on readings, they all said the same and that one was pretty much verified.

So, with power to the universe and asking the question. Whatever I am able to do to serve my country and my world I will do until the end of my days. I ask for the power to do so, the position to make it count, a lot of assistance to make it as smooth and as easy as possible. I ask for companionship from a similar being if there is such a thing here and unity for all who are like me so that we can put forward a united front here at the end of days. Amen, so shall it be, now and forever in all dimensions and in every heart. I ask for assistance, I ask for the chance to make a difference and I ask for all that it will take to save this ball of earth and its inhabitants spinning in the vastness of space until I take that ship of light and return home to my own people. It may be Aldebaran, it may be the Plaedes (seven sisters). I'd always had the idea of seven beings here to save the world, a bit grand I know. The seven cups came to me and they sit waiting for the seven to sit around a table at the end of all this and raise a goblet to success and peace.. So shall it be… Amen.

Printed in Great Britain
by Amazon